Neil Armstrong

Young Flyer

Illustrated by Meryl Henderson

Neil Armstrong

Young Flyer

by Montrew Dunham

ALADDIN PAPERBACKS

First Aladdin Paperbacks edition August 1996
Text copyright © 1996 by Montrew Dunham
Illustrations copyright © 1996 by Meryl Henderson

Aladdin Paperbacks
An imprint of Simon & Schuster
Children's Publishing Division
1230 Avenue of the Americas
New York, NY 10022

The text of this book was set in New Caledonia

Printed and bound in the United States of America

17 19 20 18 16

Library of Congress Cataloging-in-Publication Data
Dunham, Montrew
Neil Armstrong / Montrew Dunham.
p.   cm. — (Childhood of famous Americans series)
Summary: Presents the childhood of the astronaut who became
the first man to walk on the moon.
ISBN 0-689-80995-6
1. Armstrong, Neil, 1930—Juvenile literature. 2. Astronauts—United
States—Biography—Juvenile literature. [1. Armstrong, Neil, 1930—
Childhood and youth. 2. Astronauts.] I. Title. II. Series.
TL789.85.A75D86   1996
629.45'0092—dc20
[B]
96-19086

Dedicated to my grandchildren
Mackenzie, Sara, Lauren, Griffin, and Graham.

Illustrations

Numerous smaller illustrations

Contents

Neil Armstrong

Young Flyer

The Tin Goose

NEIL ARMSTRONG WAS six years old when he had his first airplane ride in the Ford Tri-Motor plane, but he had been interested in planes and flying long before that!

When Neil was only two years old his father had taken him to the National Air Show to watch the airplane races at the Cleveland airport. He loved planes from that moment on.

Neil's father, Stephen Armstrong, worked for the state of Ohio, visiting towns to look at their financial records. He had many friends who also did this same kind of work. When they were finished in one town, they all moved on to another to begin again.

Neil's family lived in Cleveland when Neil was very young. While they were there, his father would often take him to the airport to watch the planes taking off and landing. Four years later the Armstrong family moved to Warren, Ohio.

One Sunday morning in July of 1936, Mr. Armstrong said, "I understand that there is a very interesting plane coming into the airport this morning."

Viola Armstrong, Neil's mother, was setting the breakfast out on the kitchen table. Neil and his three-year-old sister, June, were sitting at the table, and baby brother Dean was in his high chair.

Mrs. Armstrong placed a large plate of scrambled eggs with bacon on the table and poured orange juice for the children. Mr. Armstrong served the two older children while Mrs. Armstrong placed Dean's food on the tray of his high chair.

"Is it a small plane?" Neil asked.

"No, as a matter of fact, it's a very big plane, made of metal," his father said.

"Does it have a name?"

"Yes. It's a Ford Tri-Motor, but it's called the Tin Goose."

"The Tin Goose? Why?"

"Because some people think it looks like tin, and it's shaped a little like a big flying goose. It's actually made of aluminum, not tin. Aluminum is a ridged metal, and makes the plane very strong."

"How many people can go up in it at one time?" Neil asked.

"About twelve passengers . . . perhaps even fourteen," his father said.

"How fast will it go?"

Mr. Armstrong smiled as he answered Neil's questions. "I believe about one hundred miles an hour, maybe even a little faster . . . one hundred and ten or so."

Neil's eyes widened as he thought about how fast that would be . . . and how exciting!

"Can we go see it?" Neil asked.

"I heard that it will be taking off for Columbus, Ohio, shortly after noon. It will probably be gone by the time we get home from church," his father said.

Mrs. Armstrong didn't stop feeding baby Dean, but she could see Neil out of the corner of her eyes. He didn't say anything. He just dropped his head and looked at his plate. His mouth drew down in disappointment.

Mrs. Armstrong looked up at the clock. "It's eight o'clock. If you can be dressed by eight-thirty, you would have time to go out to the airport for nearly an hour before Sunday school and church. That is, if your father is willing to take you."

She tightened her mouth to keep her smile from showing. She knew that Mr. Armstrong wanted to see the plane as much as Neil did.

14

"Can we go, Dad?" Neil asked as he hopped up from the table.

"Have you finished your breakfast?"

Neil nodded.

"Get dressed, then, and we'll go."

Mr. Armstrong smiled at his wife. He was glad she understood how much Neil wanted to see the big plane. "We'll be back in time for church. We'll meet you there."

The Armstrongs went to church every Sunday, and Mrs. Armstrong taught Sunday school.

Neil dressed quickly and ran back into the kitchen, his blue eyes shining. "Can we go right now?"

His father laughed. "Well, not this very minute. Let me finish my breakfast."

Neil could hardly wait.

"All right, Neil, let's go," his father said finally.

As they walked onto the airfield, Neil saw

the big plane with its three engines sitting on the runway. It was enormous!

As they walked around it, Neil looked up to see every part of the plane. He looked at the graceful propeller blades on each of the three engines, the round, fat tires on the landing wheels, and the name Ford Motor on the tail assembly.

One of the pilots came up to them. "Good morning," he said cheerfully, and put out his hand to shake Mr. Armstrong's hand. "Have you ever seen a Tin Goose?"

"No, not up close like this," Neil's father answered.

"Would you like to take a short ride this morning?"

Mr. Armstrong looked at Neil. "What about it, Neil? Would you like to go for a ride in this airplane?"

"Oh, yes." Neil thought about the planes he had watched at the Cleveland airport, streaking across the sky. Neil couldn't

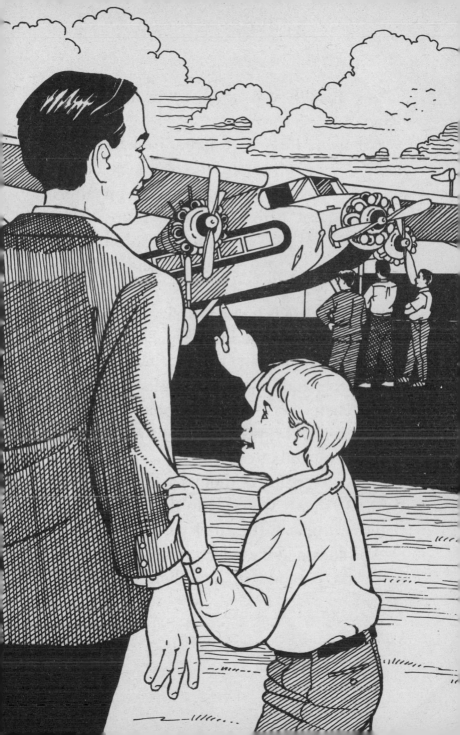

believe that he was going up in a real air-plane.

"Come on, then." His father took his hand and they climbed aboard the plane. Neil took a window seat. Another man got on after them and sat across the aisle from Neil's father. One of the pilots came over to them.

"Fasten your seat belts," he said. "Here's some chewing gum."

Mr. Armstrong helped Neil with his seat belt and then fastened his own.

"You know, when I first flew the Tin Goose, they didn't have seat belts," the pilot said. "There were only handholds that you could grip if the ride got bumpy. The seat belts are much better."

The pilot handed them each a piece of gum. He said it would help the pressure on their eardrums as they took off and landed.

"Would you like some cotton to put in your ears?" the pilot asked. "The flight gets pretty noisy."

Neil shook his head. Mr. Armstrong said he didn't need any, either.

"Well, if you are all set for an exciting ride, we'll get this plane up in the air!"

Neil took a deep breath and looked out the window at the airfield. He heard a loud squealing sound. "What is that?"

"We are getting ready to go," his father answered. "A mechanic, or maybe one of the pilots, is cranking the engines." They heard a high whining noise as the engine started to turn. Then they heard another squealing noise followed by a high whine. Finally, the third engine was wound up to a whine that signaled the engine was running. All three propellers were whirling about!

"I don't understand how they start the engines," Neil said.

"The mechanic puts a crank into the engine, and when the pilot gives him a signal, he starts turning it. This makes the propeller turn, and that usually is enough to start the gine if the pilot is quick with the throttle."

The noise was so loud that Neil could barely hear what his father was saying. The large plane rolled down the runway to get into position for takeoff. Neil was so excited, he could hardly sit still.

Suddenly, the three engines roared in a great burst of power, and the plane raced down the runway. It went faster and faster until the wheels lifted off the ground. The plane was flying!

Neil could hardly believe it! He looked out the window to see the ground slipping away below them. It didn't really feel as if the plane was moving. Neil chewed his gum faster and faster and held on to the wicker seat.

Neil's father noticed the other man in the seat across the aisle. His face was turning pale and he looked as if he was feeling sick. Mr. Armstrong looked carefully at Neil. "Do you feel all right?"

"Oh, yes!" Neil's fair skin was a little pink from the heat and excitement, but his eyes were clear and blue. He looked like he had never felt better. "We're really flying!"

The plane flew higher and higher into the blue sky. White fluffy clouds drifted alongside them. Neil kept looking out the window. He saw Mosquito Creek shining in the sunlight as it wandered through the squares of farm fields. The green and gold squares looked like one of Grandmother's quilts.

Houses looked like toys set randomly throughout the land, and every now and then a toy car drove along. The plane quickly over-took the little cars as it sped through the air.

Neil looked to the front of the plane, where the two pilots were sitting in the cockpit. He wished he knew how they were flying it.

Without warning the plane dropped with a mighty bump, and Neil felt his heart thump in his throat. The plane tilted to the right as it turned, throwing Neil toward his father. It

21

was all very exciting. Neil pulled himself up so that he could look out the window again. The edge of the horizon looked as if it were tilting, too. The plane shuddered and righted itself.

Neil didn't want the flight to end. With every turn he hoped they weren't going back to the airport. Finally, though, the Tin Goose swung around and headed toward the airport at Warren. It was then that Neil noticed the man in the seat across from his father. He looked miserable. Neil could not understand why.

"Is the ride almost over?" the man groaned.

Neil's father answered sympathetically, "I think we are on our way back to the airport."

"It can't be over too soon for me!"

"Is this your first flight?" Mr. Armstrong asked.

"Yes, and I think it's my last. I don't think I was made for flying. My stomach is turned upside down."

Neil leaned forward to look at the man. He just couldn't imagine anyone not enjoying this wonderful plane ride.

Soon they approached the airport, and the Ford Tri-Motor plane started its descent. It seemed like the plane was going too fast. Neil's father felt a little panic as the plane came closer and closer to the ground, still traveling at around sixty-five or seventy miles an hour. He could see the copilot clutching and pulling on a long bar that put on the hydraulic brakes. Mr. Armstrong had a terrible feeling that the plane was going to fall apart in midair! For a horrible moment, he wished he had not brought Neil on the flight.

They hit the ground with a thud and rolled to a stop. Mr. Armstrong put his arm around Neil to comfort him, but when he looked at Neil's face, he saw nothing but joy.

Neil and his father stayed at the airport to look at the plane. Mr. Armstrong talked with the pilots as Neil listened.

Suddenly, Neil's father looked at his watch. "Oh, Neil, we have stayed so long, we've missed church."

They hurried back home and got there just as Mrs. Armstrong was walking down the street from church with June and Dean. She started to ask them why they hadn't made it, when Neil ran up to her.

"Mom! We got to fly in the Tin Goose!" he shouted.

Mr. Armstrong looked a little sheepish. Though he felt bad that they had missed church, the flight had been so much fun. "I'm sorry. The time got away from me."

Mrs. Armstrong looked into Neil's radiant face, smiled, and decided it was all right that they had missed church.

The First Plane

Summer passed quickly. Mr. Armstrong and Neil went out to the airport sometimes to see the planes, but the Tin Goose did not come back. One day when Neil was in town with his mother, he saw a little model airplane in the window of the small hobby shop.

"Oh, Mom, look! Can we go inside to look at the airplane?"

Mrs. Armstrong stopped to look at the model in the window. "Neil, I don't think that is a plane you can buy. I believe that you buy a kit and then you make the plane."

"Can we go in to see, please?" Neil asked.

They asked the clerk in the shop. He said that the plane was built from a kit. It cost ten cents.

"Mom, can we buy it, please?"

"Do you think you could make the plane from this kit?"

"Oh, yes, I am sure I could!" Neil replied.

He was delighted. As soon as he got home, he started building the plane.

Neil took out all the pieces. He fitted the soft balsa wood together to make the plane, and then he attached the wheels with spindly wires. The little model plane had only one small propeller, not three like the big Ford Tri-Motor.

Neil still thought often about the flight he had taken. He looked at his little model plane sitting on his dresser. How nice it would be if it could really fly!

Neil snuggled down into his nice warm bed. It had been such a long time since his exciting airplane ride on that hot July day.

Neil felt sleepy. He thought back to that very special day when he and his father had flown in the big plane. He closed his eyes and could feel the rolling and pitching of the Tin Goose. He relived the flight until he finally fell asleep.

Neil awakened with a start from a dream! He sat up in bed . . . he felt like he was about to fly. The dream had been so real! He had dreamed that when he held his breath, he could float above the ground. Nothing else happened; he just floated.

Slowly, he began to realize that it was only a dream. Neil felt a little disappointed.

Neil heard the sound of voices. His mother and father must still have been awake. He hopped out of bed and went down to the living room. His parents were sitting in front of the radio, listening to a broadcast.

Neil's father turned as he saw him and extended his arms to Neil to come sit on his lap. Neil looked at his mother, who smiled gently at him. "Who is it?" he asked as he heard the soft, steady voice coming from the radio.

His mother answered quietly. "It is the King of England. Listen, now, and I will tell you about it later."

The date was December 11, 1936, and King Edward VIII was speaking from Windsor Castle in England.

Neil listened carefully. He wondered how they could hear someone so clearly who was so far away. His father commented in a low voice on the marvel of the radio. It could bring a historic event to the world at the very moment it was happening.

King Edward's voice was soft as he talked about his sense of duty to his country and the empire. But he couldn't carry on his duties as king without the support of the woman he loved. His brother would become king.

"And now we all have a new king," he said. "I wish him and you, his people, happiness and prosperity with all my heart. God bless you all. God save the King."

"What does he mean?"

Neil's parents looked at each other. His father looked thoughtful as he answered. "This is a historic moment. England now has a new ruler, King George VI. King Edward will no longer be king. Interesting that King Edward is the only king who has flown in an airplane."

"Will the new king fly in airplanes?" Neil asked.

"Oh, I am sure he will. The English Empire is so large and spread out across the world, traveling by airplane saves much time when he visits all the far-off places."

Neil's mother frowned and rested her chin on her hand. "I find it hard to understand how he could give up the throne of England when he has spent his whole life preparing to be its king. What a difficult decision for him to make." She turned to Neil. "It's so late. It's

30

time for you to go back to bed. We'll talk more about this tomorrow."

The next day, Mrs. Buller was visiting his mother when Neil came home from school. Her husband, Glenn Buller, worked with Neil's father. They all went into the kitchen, where his mother gave him some cookies and a glass of milk. Mrs. Buller and his mother continued their conversation about the abdication speech of King Edward.

Neil was very polite. He waited until there was a lull in the conversation so that he was not interrupting. "What does abdication mean?" he asked.

"That means one is giving up something. In this case, King Edward is giving up his rights to the throne of England," his mother answered.

"Is the new king the king of England right now?"

"Yes, I believe so."

"And where will the old king go?"

"He really isn't an old king, Neil. He was only the king for about a year."

"Did he become king when the last king abdicated?"

"No," his mother answered patiently. "The king before him was his father, and when his father died, Edward became king. "

"What does a king do?" Neil asked.

"Well, in a way, he rules the country. But there are other people who help him. In England, there is a prime minister, who is a little like our president. They have a Parliament, which is similar to our Congress. They all work together."

"Why did he want to quit being a king?"

"He wanted to marry a lady whom he could not marry if he were king."

"Why not?"

"She is a divorced woman, and the king is not allowed to marry a woman who is divorced," his mother answered.

Mrs. Buller smiled. "You are so patient with Neil's questions."

"He wants to know," Mrs. Armstrong answered. "And he learns by asking questions. There are never too many for me, though sometimes I don't know all the right answers."

Neil finished his cookies and milk. He left the table and went to the bookcase, where he pulled out a book. He lay down on the floor to read.

He was reading about Wilbur and Orville Wright, brothers who had invented the first successful airplane. They had lived in Dayton, Ohio, which was not very far from Wapakoneta, where his grandparents lived.

The book was so interesting that he didn't hear Mrs. Buller ask his mother, "Isn't that book a very difficult one for a first grader?" He didn't even hear his mother's answer that he read so well, this book wasn't difficult for him at all.

He learned that the Wright brothers had had a small bicycle shop in Dayton when they became interested in flying. After experimenting with a five-foot biplane kite, in 1900, they took their first man-carrying glider to Kitty Hawk, North Carolina. In 1901, they took a second glider. Neither of these gliders had flown as the brothers had hoped they would. So they went back to their shop, set up a six-foot wind tunnel, and started experi-

THE WRIGHT BROTHERS

menting with different models. From their experiments, they were able to solve the problems of balancing in flight. In the fall of 1903, they built an airplane that cost less than one thousand dollars. The plane had wings forty feet long, and it weighed, with the pilot, about 750 pounds. The Wright brothers also designed and built a lightweight gasoline engine for the plane. On December 17, 1903, Orville Wright piloted the first flight in a power-driven, heavier-than-air machine at Kitty Hawk, North Carolina.

Neil was still absorbed in his reading about the Wright Brothers when his father came in from work. Mr. Armstrong opened the front door, stomped his feet on the doormat, and shook the snow from his overcoat before hanging it up.

He greeted his wife and kissed little June and hugged baby Dean. He walked over to Neil, still stretched out on the floor with his book, and rubbed Neil's head. "What are you reading?"

"Dad, did you know about the Wright brothers?"

Mr. Armstrong smiled and nodded. "Yes, a little. What have you learned about them?"

"They invented the first airplane to fly."

"That's right. And did you know they lived right here in Ohio?"

"Do they still live here?"

"Wilbur Wright died a number of years ago, but Orville Wright still lives in Dayton. He still works on aviation in his own shop there."

"Orville Wright was the pilot of that first flight," Neil said.

"Wilbur flew some of the flights that day. There were four in all. The longest flight was a little under a minute."

Neil thought about how long he and his father had flown in the big Tri-Motor plane.

A Special Trip

THE PRETTY TEACHER stood in the front of the classroom. The golden summer sunshine bathed the shining green leaves of the trees outside. A soft June breeze came through the open windows.

Neil sat in his seat with his schoolbooks stacked on his desk in front of him. All the boys and girls waited quietly for their teacher to speak.

She looked around the room at all the first graders and smiled. "Boys and girls, we have had such a good year together in first grade. Now it's time to say good-bye. I am going to hand out your report cards, and then you may go. I do wish you all a happy summer!"

Neil walked home from school. He held his report card tightly in his hand and carried his schoolbooks under his arm.

He liked school, but he was glad it was over. Summer was so much fun. The family was planning to visit Grandmother and Grandfather Korspeter in Wapakoneta. They lived on a farm. There were always so many exciting things to do.

As he walked along, Neil thought about the dream he had had last winter. In it, when he held his breath he could float. He wondered if he could float now. Neil closed his eyes, took a deep breath, and held it. Nothing happened.

He thought maybe his schoolbooks were weighing him down. So he stacked them neatly on the grass beside the walk and laid his report card on top.

Neil stood straight with his hands at his sides. Again he closed his eyes and took a deep breath. Still, nothing happened, so he gave a little hop, hoping it would give him a boost off the ground. But it didn't work. He just stood there until he had to let his breath out.

"Neil, what are you doing?"

Neil opened his eyes and saw his mother with June and Dean coming toward him. Quickly he gathered up his books and ran toward his mother. "I was just trying to see if I could float."

His mother frowned a little. "What do you mean?"

"Oh, nothing. Never mind."

They all walked home together.

"Do you have your report card, Neil?" Mrs. Armstrong asked.

Neil held it out to his mother. "We'll look at it when we get home. Did you pass first grade?"

"I think so," Neil answered.

His mother leaned down and put her arm around his shoulder. "Of course you did. I was only teasing."

Neil ran down the sidewalk toward home

with June and Dean. Mrs. Armstrong walked along behind them. As soon as she reached the house, they all sat down on the front porch. Neil sat on the swing beside his mother, who was opening the report card. June and Dean sat on the front steps together.

Mrs. Armstrong went over every subject and every mark. They were perfect! Then she read aloud the teacher's comment at the bottom of the card. "Neil has accomplished so much this year. His reading is excellent. He has read a total of ninety books and is reading at a third-grade level."

Neil's blue eyes grew very wide and round. "That must be a mistake. Next year I'll only be in second grade."

Mrs. Armstrong smiled. "That's right. Your teacher means that you can read as well as many children in third grade. I am very proud of you, Neil."

"When are we going to Grandmother's?" June interrupted.

"We are going to leave on Friday, just as soon as your father gets home from work."

"Are we going to stay all week?" Neil asked.

"Yes. Your father will need to come back for work on Monday, but we will stay all week and then he will return to Grandmother's the next weekend. Come, let's go in for lunch," said Mrs. Armstrong.

Neil and his sister and brother all trooped in behind their mother and sat down at the table as she set out their lunch before them. They ate their sandwiches and drank their milk. After lunch they went out to play.

Neil brought out his little balsa plane and tried to get it to fly. But it would sail for just a few feet and then tumble to the ground. Neil would pick it up, dust the dirt off, and, with a flick of the wrist, send it off again.

On Friday, each of the children had packed what they wanted to take to

Grandmother and Grandfather Korspeter's. Neil, of course, was taking his little plane and his books. June and Dean had selected their toys. They were so excited when their father finally came home that they all got into the car before he had a chance to say hello.

Mr. Armstrong loaded their suitcases in the trunk of the car as the three children sat in the back seat. Mrs. Armstrong locked the front door of the house. She was carrying a small basket with snacks for them to eat along the way. Mr. Armstrong opened the door and helped her into the front seat with her basket and closed the door. Then he went around the car and got into the driver's seat. He started the car and they were on their way!

The late afternoon was warm, and all the car windows were rolled down. The hot breeze was strong as it blew on Neil's face. Dean sat in the middle, and June sat by the other window with her hair flying in the wind.

"How soon will we be there?" Neil asked.

His mother turned her head to answer. "Oh, Neil, we have only started our trip!"

June continued the question. "When will we be there?"

"It's a very short trip. So just sit back and enjoy the ride."

"May I have a cookie? " Dean asked.

"Yes, of course," his mother said as she dipped into her basket of goodies.

At last Mr. Armstrong turned the car into the lane to their grandparents' farmhouse. He had scarcely stopped the car when Grandmother stepped out on the front porch. She was wiping off her hands on her apron as she came out to the car to greet her grandchildren. She gave them all a big hug hello.

"Come on in. Supper's on the table. Your grandfather is just coming in from the barn."

Everyone was talking at once. They had so many things to tell Grandmother. Mr. Armstrong carried in their suitcases and put them in their bedrooms. Mrs. Armstrong

took off her hat and went to the kitchen to help put the last of the things on the supper table.

When Grandfather came in, they all sat down around the big table. There was a platter heaped high with crispy fried chicken, a bowl of creamy mashed potatoes, and another with green beans. A large bowl overflowed with cole slaw and another with cottage cheese, which Grandmother called "smearcase."

They all ate and talked. Grandmother wanted to hear from all the children. June wanted to tell about the clothes she and her mother had made for her doll.

"How was school, Neil?" Grandmother asked.

"I'm out of school now . . . but I learned to read!"

"Oh, I know you did. You were reading so well when you were here in the spring!"

"I'm going to be in second grade when I go back to school in September."

"Yes, and it will be in a new school," his father added.

"Are you going to be moving again?" Grandfather asked.

"Yes, we've finished our work, so we'll be moving on to a new county to work on their records. We'll probably move at the end of August," Mr. Armstrong answered.

"This will be our sixth move," Mrs. Armstrong said. "But Stephen has a good job, and moving is a part of the job. Besides, we always enjoy where we live."

After dinner Neil and June went outside to play. There was a large grassy lawn, and the outdoors just smelled so good.

All too soon, their mother called and said it was time for bed.

The sun, which was setting in the west, was a flaming orange ball, and the sky above it was just beginning to turn a rich shade of lavender. "But it isn't even dark yet," Neil protested.

Mrs. Armstrong came out and sat on the step with June and Neil. They watched the sun dip out of sight and the sky darken. Finally, when the sky was completely dark, they went in to bed. Dean was already sound asleep. Mrs. Armstrong tucked June and Neil in and kissed them good night.

Neil nestled down between the smooth, sun-dried sheets and rolled over to look out the window. The sky had become velvety dark with all the twinkling stars. The air was so fresh, and the only sounds were those of crickets. He felt happy as he fell asleep.

Great-Grandfather Koetter

THE DAYS AT the farm were happy ones. There were so many different things to do. Neil could run and play and do whatever he wanted. He went out to the barn with his grandfather when he fed the animals. He wandered through the cornfield where the fresh, green sprouts of corn were growing. They were only six or eight inches tall, but it seemed every day they grew a little more. Grandmother said if he listened at night he could hear them growing.

Neil especially liked to ride their pony,

though he always had to ask permission first from an adult.

One Saturday morning after breakfast, Neil went out with his father to ride the pony. He watched as his father saddled her up. She stood very quietly as he fastened the cinch strap around her belly, placed the bit in her mouth, and put the reins back over her head.

Then Neil put his foot in the stirrup and swung up into the saddle. With a "giddyap," off they went, jogging down the path. The pony went at her own pace, which wasn't very fast. Neil rode down the lane as his father stood in the barnyard watching him. Then Neil wheeled the pony around and rode back.

June came skipping out of the house and cried, "It's my turn! Can I ride the pony?"

"One more trip down the lane, Neil, and then June gets a turn," his father called.

Neil rode down to the road and back again. He really wasn't ready to get off. "Can I ride again after June has her turn?"

His father nodded. "June can ride down the lane two times just as you did, then we'll let Dean have a short ride."

Finally it was Neil's turn again. Mr. Armstrong held the reins, and Neil hopped up into the saddle. "May I ride through the fields?"

"Yes, as long as you are careful and don't allow the pony to step on any of the new corn plants," replied his father.

Neil squeezed his legs gently against the pony's sides and pulled gently on the reins to head the pony toward the fields.

They walked through the corn rows to the fence, turned right, and went along the fence back to the barn. His father was still there, and he opened the gate so that Neil and the pony could go into the back fields where there was a meadow. Neil rode round and round. He thought about how the Indians used to ride their ponies here, too, through the woods and meadows and down by the creek.

It was nearly noon when he came back to the barnyard. He pulled the pony up by the fence and climbed down. He led her back to her stall in the barn and carefully removed the saddle and bridle.

Neil went through the screen door into the summer kitchen. This was a small kitchen at the back of the house. It was used during the hottest part of summer so the rest of the house didn't get too hot from all the cooking. He then went on into the family kitchen, where his grandmother was making bread. He loved to sit at the kitchen table and talk with Grandmother as she made bread. She would place a large batch of dough on the wooden table, which had been scrubbed white, and then she would knead the dough with her hands. "Did you have a good ride?"

"Oh, yes. I rode through the meadows and even down by the creek."

"Do you know that Indians used to live on

this land? They rode their ponies the same places you did." Grandmother said.

Neil nodded. He listened as she told him about the days when Indians lived in Ohio and people from Europe came to settle there.

Many of the settlers in the Ohio area came from Germany, where there were wars and young men were forced to join the army. They wanted to live peacefully and have farms and families.

Neil had heard about his own great-grandfather, but he liked to hear the story again. "Your great-grandfather Koetter settled on a farm here in Ohio in the 1860s," Grandmother told him.

Grandmother rolled the dough and turned it over. With the heel of her hand she punched down the dough. She divided it into smaller sections and placed each section in a bread pan. She set the pans on top of the stove to let the dough rise.

She told Neil about her father, Neil's great-grandfather, as she placed the pans on the stove. "Fritz Wilhelm Koetter was born in August 1846, over ninety years ago, in Ladbergen, Germany. When he was eighteen years old, he did not want to serve in the Prussian Army, so he decided to come to the United States."

"How did he know that he wanted to come to Ohio?" Neil asked.

"I don't really know," Grandmother answered. "There were many people who came from Germany to Ohio. Perhaps he knew some people who had already come here, and they had written about the good farmland. Nonetheless, he started on his way. He boarded a ship to cross the Atlantic Ocean. In those days it was a long, difficult voyage. Many of the passengers became very sick. The ship was at sea for six weeks or so before it reached New York harbor."

"Was he all by himself?"

"I'm not sure, but I think he was.

"After he had been gone three days," Grandmother continued, "and his father knew that he was safely out of Germany, he reported to the police that his son was missing!"

"You mean when he knew they could not find him!"

"That's right." Grandmother sat down at the kitchen table with Neil. "He came in through immigration at New York City."

"Is that Ellis Island?" Neil asked. "I read a story about Ellis Island and people who came into the United States through there."

"No, I believe he entered through the immigration station at Castle Garden, which was open before Ellis Island. Then he had to make his way to Ohio. I don't know whether he took a coach or rode horseback, but he probably came out on the old National Road." Grandmother thought a moment, "You know, he might have come by boat on Lake Erie. I don't really know."

Neil listened with interest to his grandmother. She always told great stories. She went on to say, "Grandfather Koetter settled in Ohio, and our family has been here ever since."

"Did he ever go back home to Germany?" Neil asked.

"No," Grandmother answered. "He never saw his mother and father again. Can you imagine how it would be to go to a strange land all by yourself?"

Neil was quiet for a few moments. He wondered how that would feel.

"Well, that's enough about Grandfather Koetter for now. How would you like to have a picnic lunch? Go find June and Dean, and we'll have lunch outside under the big oak tree."

Grandmother filled her picnic basket with cold fried chicken, sliced apples, and cookies. She made a big pitcher of frosty lemonade, and they all gathered around the picnic table. There were three drumsticks, one for each child.

Neil's father laughed, "That must have been a three-legged chicken! I've never heard of such a thing!"

The grown-ups went on into the house for their lunch. After they were finished eating, Neil and June put the leftovers and dirty plates in the basket. June and Dean climbed down from the picnic bench and ran to play.

Neil tried to drag the basket into the house by himself, but his mother saw him and came out to help. She also took in the lemonade pitcher.

"May I make one of my model planes now?" Neil asked.

"Wouldn't you like to play with June and Dean?" his mother asked.

"I will after a while, but I have the neatest model I'd like to build. Then we can play with it later."

"All right. Do you know where your model airplane kit is?"

Neil nodded. He ran to his room to get the

kit. He took it out to the picnic table to put it together. He was very careful as he opened the cardboard box. He laid out each part of the plane neatly.

Neil carefully glued the parts together and put the markings on the plane. When it was finished, he left it on the table so the glue could dry.

After supper, as dusk was falling, he took the plane out on the front lawn. His grandparents and parents sat on the porch as Neil, June, and Dean played on the lawn.

Neil wound up the little rubber-band motor. Then, holding his model plane aloft, he sent it off with a swing of his arm. The light plane glided on the breeze and then fell to the ground. Dean laughed as he ran to catch it and bring it back to Neil. Neil sailed the plane again. Usually the little plane would hardly fly at all before falling to the ground. But sometimes when it caught the breeze just right, it would glide along.

The long summer evening gradually darkened into night, and the spacious lawn became dotted with lightning bugs. June and Dean lost interest in the plane as they ran to catch the gleaming fireflies. But Neil continued flying his plane.

He ran after the plane until he could hardly see it sailing through the darkness.

The Wolf Patrol

THAT FALL NEIL entered his new school. But, because he read so well, he was placed in the third grade instead of the second. When he read to his new teacher, she had him read more and more difficult books. Finally, she told Mrs. Armstrong that Neil could read at the fifth-grade level!

Neil's mother was pleased, but not really surprised, because she and Neil had read so many books together. Mrs. Armstrong loved to read and spent many hours reading with all her children.

Neil did well in his new school. He read more and more about planes and flying. He read magazines about airplanes, and he kept a scrapbook, cutting out pictures of planes and saving them in it.

When Neil was in sixth grade, his family moved again. This time to Upper Sandusky, Ohio. Neil made many friends there. Two of his best friends were Konstantin Solacoff, called Kotcho for short, and Bud Blackford. Neil still enjoyed building model airplanes, and the other boys did, also. After they built their models, they would go out and fly them together. Sometimes they went up to Neil's room on the second floor and flew them out the window.

Neil needed money to buy the model plane kits. He heard that the caretaker at Mission Cemetery was looking for boys to mow the grass, so he went to talk to the caretaker to see if he could get a job.

"Yes, that's right, we need the grass

mowed. You would have to mow at least once a week. Would you have time to do that with school and all?"

"Oh, yes, I could mow after school. When school is out, I could work any day you wanted me to."

"You look a little small. It takes a good strong push to run this lawn mower."

"I'm really strong. I mow the grass at home," Neil replied.

"Well, okay. You've got the job. The pay is ten cents an hour. If you do a good job, we might go up to fifteen cents an hour."

"Thanks!"

Neil ran home to tell his parents that he had gotten a job. His father had just come home from work, and his mother was in the kitchen fixing dinner.

"Mom! Dad! I got a job," Neil shouted as he ran in the back door.

His father smiled. "You got a job? Where?"

Neil told him that he was going to cut the

grass in Mission Cemetery. His parents looked at each other.

"How often will you have to work?" his father asked.

"Just once a week most of the time, unless the grass grows very fast. I can do it on Saturday, or after school . . . and then any day this summer."

Neil's father walked over to him and patted him on the shoulder. "I'm proud of you. When you want money, you are willing to work for it."

That summer went quickly for Neil. His job, his airplane magazines, his model planes, and his friends kept him very busy.

Autumn came and was filled with clear, crisp days of blue skies and white clouds. The large oak trees and vivid maple trees were clad in their glorious fall colors of gold and scarlet. Soon winter winds began to blow, and the leaves fell to the ground.

On December 7, 1941, the peace of the whole country was shattered: The Japanese bombed Pearl Harbor! The Armstrongs were shocked when the news came over the radio. They listened closely as President Franklin Delano Roosevelt declared that the country was at war!

At first, Neil and his friends had difficulty understanding what the war would mean to the country. They talked among themselves, and they listened to what their parents were saying. They really thought the war would be over soon. The United States was so strong that it wouldn't take long to defeat the Japanese.

At the beginning, the war didn't make too much difference to the boys in Upper Sandusky, though they could see some changes around them. Older brothers were being drafted into the army, and many young men joined all the branches of the armed forces. Gas was rationed so they couldn't see

Grandmother and Grandfather Korspeter very often. Meat and food were also rationed, but Neil's mother was such a good cook that they always had delicious meals. In most ways, though, Neil's and his friends' lives didn't change.

There was no Boy Scout troop when Neil first moved to Upper Sandusky. But after a year or so, a troop was organized. Kotcho, Bud, and Neil were among the first members of Troop #25. Eddie Nause was the Scoutmaster, and Neil's father was the Assistant Scoutmaster.

The troop met in a large hall over the Commercial Bank once a month. Their Wolf Patrol met every week in the members' homes as they worked on their requirements to become Tenderfoot Scouts. The other boys in their patrol were Dick Tucher, Jack Stecher, and Jack Strasser. Neil was the patrol scribe.

Time passed quickly as they learned the

many skills they needed for their Boy Scout requirements. One hot summer day, Neil, Kotcho, and Bud got out their handbooks and read what they needed to do to pass their second- and first-class scouting. They learned about all the badges they needed to earn.

"Why don't we go out to Reber Woods? We can hike and work on our maps," Neil suggested. He and his friends loved to ride their bikes out to Reber Woods, where they could hike.

"That's a great idea!" Bud replied. "Let's ride our bikes out there today."

"We should take our lunches so we can stay there all day," Kotcho said enthusiastically.

The boys decided that each would go to his own house, pack his lunch, and get his gear. They would meet back at Neil's house before setting off to the woods.

Neil's mother packed his lunch while he filled his canteen with water. He got his Boy

Scout handbook and a pencil and paper for mapmaking and put them into his pack. Finally, he clipped his Boy Scout knife onto his belt.

His mother smiled. "You look like you are ready for anything."

"You know the Boy Scout motto, Mom!" Neil laughed. "'Be prepared!'"

The boys rode their bikes over the dusty road. They pedaled as fast as they could, passing one another as they raced along. They felt like they were really on an expedition. Neil was in the lead. As he turned onto the path that led into the woods, he had to slow down because it was narrow and bumpy. He came to a little clearing and he slammed on his brakes, skidding to a stop. Bud and Kotcho were right behind him.

"Let's put our bikes back in the underbrush so no one will see them," Bud said.

"Who's going to see them? There's no one else here," Kotcho retorted.

"It might be a good idea," Neil said. "Then the bikes will be out of our way."

After they stowed the bikes back away from the clearing, the boys sat down around a flat stone where they could get out their books and make their plans.

"Let's work on mapmaking first," Neil suggested. "I'll find a path through the woods and make a map, and one of you can try to follow it."

"That's good," Bud replied. "But why don't each of us take a trail through the woods and make a map? Then we can trade maps to see if we can follow the other guy's trail."

"Okay, that's a good idea. But why don't we eat our lunches first and then do our hiking?" Kotcho asked.

Bud stood up. "We don't need to eat yet. We just got here!"

"All right," Kotcho agreed grudgingly. "Let's go, but I'm taking my canteen with me. I'm thirsty, and if I get lost, I want to have my water with me!"

They set off, each in a different direction. Neil went toward the river. Though the sun was hot, the slight wind through the trees cooled the air in the woods.

Neil walked along carefully, trying not to step on the twigs underfoot so that he wouldn't make any noise.

His canteen was slung over his shoulder. He stopped to unscrew the cap and take a drink of the cool water. He had his pencil and his paper ready, and every now and then he would drop to one knee and write on his map.

After he had completed his map going down to the river and back again, he returned to the small clearing. Kotcho was already there with his completed map, and within minutes Bud came walking in with his.

"Should we have our lunch now?" Kotcho asked. "Then we can trade maps. I'll take Neil's, Neil can take Bud's, and Bud can take mine."

"That'll work!" Neil said.

"Let's eat!" Bud said.

They all sat on the ground and spread their lunches in front of them. They were very hungry after their four-mile bike ride from town and their hike through the woods. After they had finished their sandwiches and fruit, Neil brought out a large bag of cookies that his mother had packed.

"Boy, those cookies look good," Bud said.

Neil grinned. "I'm sharing. Mom sent enough for all of us."

"Your mom makes the best cookies," Kotcho said.

As soon as they were finished, they gathered up their trash and put it in their knapsacks so that they would leave the woods just as they had found it. They exchanged maps and went on their map-following hike.

Neil followed Bud's map. It was drawn very carefully. It led him down into a very dark thicket. He could hardly find his way through to the other side.

Bud's map was easy to follow, but Neil got out his compass anyway, just to see which direction he was going. The path kept doubling back with sharp turns.

He was heading away from the river. The path he had taken before lunch had gone the opposite way, toward the river.

Neil finally reached his destination: an enormous oak tree. He had done it, and without any trouble. Neil sat down at the base of the tree and took a drink of water from his canteen.

He wondered how the other boys were doing with their maps. After a few minutes he got up and started back.

Neil was the first to return. Bud and Kotcho came in right after him. They were all happy that they had made maps that could be read and followed with no difficulty.

"Wouldn't this be a great place to camp?" Neil asked. "I was thinking we could bring our tents."

"Yeah! We could build a campfire and cook our food. We could take hikes, and study the stars at night, and work on our merit badges. Wouldn't that be super!" Bud said. Kotcho agreed.

The boys started to make their plans. They were really excited! They gathered up their knapsacks, pulled their bikes out, and rode home to get permission from their parents.

Camping Out

THE BOYS RODE back to town as fast as they could to prepare for their camp out. They met at Neil's house since Neil's father was the Assistant Scoutmaster.

"Hey, Dad! We have a great idea," Neil said excitedly. "We want to camp at Reber Woods and complete our requirements to be first-class Scouts!"

Mr. Armstrong nodded. "You do, do you? Tell me about your plans."

Kotcho answered, "We'll take our tents and bedrolls and sleep out. We'll build a

campfire and cook our supper and breakfast." He pulled out his Boy Scout handbook.
"We'll complete our camping and cooking
skill awards, and earn a hiking badge . . . and
work on our knots!"

"When do you plan to do this?" Mr.
Armstrong asked.

"Tomorrow night," Neil replied.

"Then you have a good deal of work to do
before your outing," Mr. Armstrong said in a
matter-of-fact voice. "First, you say you want
to camp in Reber Woods? Shouldn't you get
Mr. Reber's permission first?"

"It'll be all right with him," Bud answered
quickly. "He always lets us hike there."

"It probably is all right with him, but one
of you boys should ask his permission, anyway."

Mr. Armstrong helped the boys think of all
the things they would need. He also suggested
that the three of them share responsibility for
getting ready for the overnight trip.

They were all excited as they divided up the jobs. Kotcho would talk to Mr. Reber down at the bank. Bud would do the grocery shopping for their supper and breakfast. And Neil would get the hatchet they would need for setting up camp and making their campfire. Each of them would get his own gear together, their pup tents, bedrolls, and cooking equipment. They agreed to start out right after lunch the next day.

After Kotcho and Bud had left, Neil went down in the basement to get a small hatchet. When he ran his finger across the surface, he decided it needed sharpening. He used his father's stone, just as he had been taught in the Scouts.

While Neil was in the basement, Mrs. Armstrong sat down by her husband. "Are you sure this is a good idea?"

"What do you mean?" Mr. Armstrong asked.

"I know the boys are very responsible, but

I worry about them being alone and having a campfire."

Mr. Armstrong gently placed his hand over his wife's as he reassured her. "Of course they will be all right. They have learned the right way to build a fire. They know how to use the hatchet to cut firewood. This is learning in the best Boy Scout tradition. "

Neil's mother smiled. "I know that . . . it's just . . ."

"It's a good time for them to explore and learn to be self-reliant," Mr. Armstrong said confidently.

The next morning the three boys were very busy getting ready for their camp out. Kotcho rode his bike down to the bank and went in to see Mr. Reber, the bank president. He walked to the back of the bank and asked the secretary if he could talk with Mr. Reber. The office door was open, and Mr. Reber could see Kotcho standing there. "Come on in," he said in a welcoming voice.

Kotcho told Mr. Reber their plans and asked if it would be all right with him if they camped in his woods.

"Of course, you're welcome to go there anytime you want to," Mr. Reber answered.

"Thank you. We thought you wouldn't mind, but we wanted to be sure."

While Kotcho was visiting the bank, Bud went to the grocery store and bought the food they would need for supper and breakfast, and Neil gathered the other supplies. Besides the sharpened hatchet, he collected a small folding camp spade, some matches, cooking utensils, a small bucket, and the stakes for the pup tents. He brought salt and pepper, a little jar of sugar, some soap, and, at the last minute, put in some citronella in case there were mosquitoes. As it turned out, it was good that he remembered the citronella.

Each of the boys packed his own backpack with his tent, bedroll, clothes, and his own canteen filled with fresh water.

They set off shortly after lunch, with their fully loaded backpacks, pedaling their bicycles the four miles to the woods. Finally, they reached the trees. Climbing off their bikes, they walked them down the path into the deep woods, where it was dark and cool.

They went into the woods about a hundred yards and stopped. They rolled their backpacks off and sat down to cool off and make their plans.

"I think we need to set up camp first," Neil said.

"That's right, but we need to decide where," Bud added.

"Maybe we ought to go closer to the river," Kotcho suggested. "We'll need water for cooking and washing, and if it's very hot, we'll want to swim."

"We'll want the tents in a circle around an open area where we can build our campfire," Neil added. "Let's scope out the area to see where the best spot is."

The boys walked around and agreed on a small clearing not too far from the Sandusky River. Each boy set up his own tent, trading the hatchet back and forth as they drove the stakes into the ground. They lashed the ropes around the stakes to secure their tents.

"Should we gather firewood for the fire tonight?" Neil asked.

"It's pretty hot for a campfire," Kotcho said.

"Well, we have to have a fire to cook our supper. Besides, it's going to get cooler," Bud said. "But first we need to secure our food."

"What do you mean?" Kotcho asked.

"We need to get it off the ground, so animals can't get into it," Neil answered as he looked around for a way to do that. "I've got it! Why don't we tie two of the bicycles together against that big tree, and we can stack the food on top of them?"

"Good idea!" Bud and Kotcho agreed.

They rolled Bud's and Neil's bikes over to

the tree and, by using some of their rope-tying skills, lashed the bikes to each other and to the tree. Then they placed the sacks of food on the package racks and on the seats of the bicycles and tied them down. Bud had organized the groceries into one bag of dry foods, one bag of vegetables, a small canvas bag with the eggs, and a small package of ground beef packed in ice.

Next they needed to clear a space for the campfire. They cleared the ground of all the twigs and leaves using the camp spade.

"Let's all gather wood and then come back and decide what kind of a fire we should build," suggested Neil.

They set out in different directions. Neil collected fairly large branches that had fallen from the trees. As soon as he had an armload, he came back to the campsite and stacked them against a tree at the edge of the clearing. The other boys did the same thing, and soon they had a good stack of wood.

"Now we need some tinder and some kindling," Kotcho said. Bud gathered some dry weeds and bark that had fallen from dead trees onto the floor of the forest, while Neil and Kotcho gathered small dry twigs.

"I'll lay the fire," Neil volunteered.

"Let me build it," Kotcho said. "I need to pass fire building for my requirements."

"So do I," Neil said. "What if I build it today and you build it in the morning for breakfast?"

"Okay," Kotcho agreed.

"And I'll cook tonight," Bud said. "And you guys can make breakfast."

So Neil set about to lay the fire. He wadded up some of the dry weeds and bark and placed everything in the center for tinder. He took the dry twigs for kindling and placed them over the tinder.

"I think I'll make a hunter's fireplace with two large logs on either side to set our pots on for cooking," he said.

Bud, who was to be the cook, said, "I think it would be better to have a rock fireplace. It's easier to use level rocks to set the pot and skillet on."

"But with logs, we can have a campfire after we eat. We'll just add more logs on as these logs burn."

"All right, then, but be sure the logs are close enough together and flat enough that the pot and skillet will balance."

Neil went to the log pile and selected two wide logs and, with his hatchet, trimmed them off so they would lie flat on either side of the fire bed. He placed them close enough together so that the cooking gear would balance on both logs.

Satisfied that the fire was laid for cooking, he took the small bucket and went down to the river to get some water. He placed the bucket full of water at the outer edge of the fire ring.

The boys spent the rest of the afternoon

hiking. They practiced marking their paths with Indian trail signs. One of the boys would go ahead and mark the trail. Forked sticks meant straight ahead, sticks in a crook showed turns either to the left or the right, and two crossed sticks meant not that way. The other two would follow the trail.

At suppertime, Bud got out the food.

"Shall I light the fire now?" Neil asked. Bud said yes, so Neil took out his matches, knelt down, and set the tinder ablaze.

Bud and Neil got out their cooking kits, which consisted of small, lightweight pots and pans. There was a large flat rock at the edge of the clearing where Bud spread out the paper grocery bag. He laid out the vegetables on it. He peeled an onion, three potatoes, and some carrots and put them in his pot.

Neil and Kotcho were doing other tasks. Neil rubbed the outside of his stew pot and frying pan with soap so that they would be easy to wash afterward.

When the fire had burned down to embers, Bud put the hamburger in Neil's skillet and browned it. He put the vegetables in Neil's stew pot with some tomatoes. After the meat was browned, he added it to the stew.

The boys got their plates and forks and spread a small piece of canvas on the ground for their table. After an hour or so, Bud dished up the stew onto their plates and set out some bread. For dessert they had apples and cookies. They all agreed it was a great supper.

Kotcho washed up the plates and pots after dinner with water warmed over the fire. Neil put more logs on the campfire.

The evening turned dark as they finished all their camping chores. They sat around the campfire as the glowing embers gradually became gray and the fire died out.

They looked up at the stars in the dark sky. They could see the Big Dipper and the North Star. The boys recognized them from the chart of the heavens in their Scout handbook.

The stars shined much brighter in the darkened country sky with no lights from town to dim them.

As they talked they could hear the sounds of the forest, the harrumphing of frogs, the chirping of crickets, and the occasional snapping twig from an animal walking nearby.

As they got ready for bed, Neil checked to make sure the fire was out. He took the camp shovel and tossed a little dirt over the fire bed. He set the bucket of water right by the fire and sprinkled some water over the cold embers.

The boys climbed into their bedrolls in their little tents and settled for sleep after an exciting day in the woods.

A Scout's Pace

NEIL OPENED HIS eyes slowly. He had been dreaming again that he was floating above the ground. In his dream he had held his breath and floated. He just hovered, and then he woke up. And like the other times he'd had the dream, he felt like something ought to happen. But instead, the dream just went away.

Neil poked his head out of the tent. The morning air felt cool and fresh. The low rays of the rising sun filtered through the trees. He crawled a little way out of his bedroll.

The other boys were quiet in their tents.

Neil lay there for a little while, listening to the soft sounds of the forest. He heard the staccato pounding of a woodpecker. He saw a plump gray rabbit scamper across the clearing as a blue jay scolded from the oak tree.

Neil turned on his back so that he could look up at the sky. He thought about the velvety dark sky of the night before and how the heavens had been filled with bright stars. Now they were nowhere to be seen in the clear blue of the morning sky.

He hopped up from his tent, snatched the bucket from the fire site, and ran down to the river. Quickly he scooped fresh water into the bucket and splashed some over his face.

Kotcho and Bud joined him. They splashed one another with the water until they were all soaking wet.

"Wait a minute," Neil said, laughing. "I'm hungry. Let's start breakfast." He grabbed the bucket of water and ran back to the campsite with Kotcho and Bud right behind him.

Kotcho started to lay the fire. He spread the ashes from the previous night's fire out with the camp shovel and placed the dry tinder in the center. "I'm going to make a rock fireplace this morning. I think it's easier to cook on the flat stones."

"That's good," said Bud. "I'll look for some good flat stones."

Bud went down by the riverbank and came back carrying two fairly large flat rocks. He placed them by the fire site and went back for two more, while Kotcho was laying the kindling on top of the tinder. Soon Bud was back, and they placed two stones on each side of the firebed.

Kotcho got the matches and lit the fire. Orange flames came licking up and then settled into a steady blaze.

Neil was the chef for breakfast. He asked Bud to get a pot of water to boil for oatmeal.

He laid the food out to prepare breakfast. He cut holes out of three oranges and put them aside. Each boy could squeeze an orange and drink its juice while he was waiting for his breakfast to cook.

Neil measured out the dry oatmeal that he would cook in the boiling water.

He laid the six eggs on the rock, barricading them with the mess kits so that they wouldn't roll off. He didn't want them to break until he was ready to crack them open to make scrambled eggs. Last, he opened a package that his mother had given him, which had six of her delicious sweet rolls.

Breakfast tasted great to the hungry boys. They all decided that they had passed their cooking-skill requirements for their first-class Scout level. They also agreed that the rock fireplace worked better than the hunter's fireplace.

They all cleaned up together. They washed their cooking utensils and put each of their cooking kits back together again. The canvas bag that had held the ice cubes and the cold foods was draped over a branch to dry.

The boys spent the morning practicing their knot-tying skills until they decided to take a short hike. Each of them went a different way, taking a pencil and paper to list all the different trees, birds, and animals they saw. They were going to meet back at the camp at eleven o' clock.

Neil climbed over a large log and started to walk quietly into the woods. Looking carefully about the forest, he identified oak trees, sugar maples, a sassafras tree, and a dogwood. He recognized them by their leaves.

A chipmunk darted across the path in front of him. He heard the song of a cardinal, and as he looked in the branches overhead, he saw the muted brownish-red female. But it was not her song he heard. He looked a few feet away and saw the scarlet male cardinal in the tree.

Neil hiked and hiked through the forest. There were no paths, so he had to go between trees, over logs, and through undergrowth. He enjoyed the smells and the stillness of the woods.

Finally, the boys returned at eleven o'clock and compared what they had seen on their hikes. They each had a long list of different trees, birds, and animals.

They now needed to strike camp and go home. Each of them packed his own tent and bedroll into his backpack. Then they made sure the fire was cold and sprinkled more water on it. They moved the big cooking stones back to the edge of the clearing so that no one coming into the woods would stumble on them.

Each of the boys checked the campsite. It looked perfectly clean. It was important to leave the woods exactly as they had found it.

When Neil got home, his mother said that the caretaker had called and wanted him to mow the grass at the cemetery that afternoon. Neil started to unpack his camping gear quickly.

"I think it will be all right if you wait until after supper to mow. It should be a little cooler by then," his mother said.

"How did the camping go?" his father asked when he came in.

"Just great," Neil replied. He told about all the things they had done.

"I believe you and Bud and Kotcho need to tell Scoutmaster Nause about your camping trip. You should be able to qualify for first-class Scouts."

After supper, Neil went to the cemetery to mow. The summer breeze did cool him a little as he pushed the stiff lawn mower.

When summer was over and the grass no longer needed mowing, Neil got a job at Neumeister's Bakery. So did Bud Blackford. Neil made 110 dozen doughnuts every night!

He also had the job of cleaning out the big dough mixer with a scraper. He got that job because he was small enough to climb inside the big vat to clean it. Also, when the bakers took the fresh bread out of the ovens, Neil stacked the bread on the shelves.

He worked after school from about four o'clock in the afternoon to nine or ten at night. He didn't work on Saturdays since there was no bread delivery on Sundays, but he did work on Sundays from about two o'clock to nine or ten. Bud's hours were not the same as Neil's, because he did different work.

One Sunday, Bud, Kotcho, and Neil decided to hike to Carey, Ohio, which was about ten miles north of Upper Sandusky. They planned to eat their lunch there and then hike back. This would meet their twenty-mile hiking requirement for Boy Scouts.

The hike took longer than they had thought it would. They ate their lunch and then started back. Neil looked at the time and knew that if he did not hurry, he would be late for work at Neumeister's Bakery.

He decided to go at a Scout's pace to hurry back. "I'll see you guys later," he said to Bud and Kotcho, and he was gone.

A Scout's pace is a mixture of jogging and walking. Neil jogged about twenty-five paces at an easy dogtrot, and then walked twenty-five paces. He kept repeating the jogging and walking. He got to the bakery in the nick of time and then had to work his regular shift.

Kotcho and Bud were so tired from the twenty-mile hike, they didn't know how Neil possibly could have kept up a Scout's pace to get back to work and still have enough energy to do his job!

Winners and Losers

NEIL BENT OVER the table where he was working on his model plane. Because of World War II, balsa wood was not always easy to find for the models. He used whatever he could find to build his planes. He used scraps of wood, straw, paper, and sometimes even heavy cardboard and bits of building materials.

He no longer bought kits; he designed his models himself. With his X-Acto knife, he carefully made a cut along the line he had drawn on the piece of thin wood. He glanced at his design to make sure that he was making the cut properly. He had his design in front of him.

With careful thought he laid out his pieces of wood to be glued together. He took the lid off the glue and, very cautiously, placed droplets in the right spots. He smoothed out the ribbon of glue and, finally, put the two pieces together.

He finished gluing the plane's parts together, and set it on the back of his table to dry.

Neil then took another plane that he had put together the night before. He checked to make sure that it was completely dry and that the glue was firm and solid. He opened a little jar of paint. Taking a fine paintbrush, he dipped it into the paint and, with great pains, painted the raw wood a rich blue color.

"Neil," his mother called. "We'll be leaving for church in about twenty minutes. Are you ready to go?"

"I'm painting, but I'm almost done."

His mother laughed. She knew that Neil was at work on another of his models. Whenever he had a moment, he was at his table working on them. She always tried to call him far enough ahead of their going any-place, so that he would have time to finish what he was doing and get ready to go.

Neil finished his painting, cleaned off his brush, and set the plane aside to dry. He looked down at his paint-smeared hands and then at the clock. He needed to hurry to clean his hands and put on his church clothes. He scrambled to get into his clothes and catch up with the family, who had start-ed to walk on ahead.

The Armstrong family went to the Trinity Church, which was just a block or so down the street from where they lived. Neil's mother needed to be there promptly because she taught Sunday school. Neil, June, and Dean went to Sunday school, and then they went to church with their parents.

100

Neil was anxious to get home from church so that he could get back to his model building. He had an hour or so to work before their Sunday dinner. After dinner he wanted to go to the park with Kotcho and Bud to fly some of their planes.

Most of Neil's friends also made model planes, but his were usually better than theirs. When they flew their models, Neil's almost always flew longer and farther than his friends' planes.

Neil was very interested in airplanes. He loved to read the magazines about them, and he became very good at identifying all different kinds of aircraft.

Neil had a very busy schedule. There was the Boy Scout troop, which met once a month. In addition, the Wolf Patrol met every week so they could work on their merit badges. Neil also played in the school band with Bud, and they both continued to work at Neumeister's Bakery. There was barely enough time for Neil to do all the things he wanted to do, but he always managed to find time for planes.

Kotcho, Bud, and Neil liked school and did well in their classes. They were all good students and competed with one another to get the very best grades. In general science they were the top students in the class!

When the time came for the science fair, Neil and his friends were very excited about their projects. Bud and Kotcho decided that they would build a photoelectric cell. They would shine a light on the cell and make electricity. Neil decided that he would do his own project for the science fair.

Each of the boys spent hours working on their projects. Bud and Kotcho had to mix chemicals over two or three weeks and let them stand for several days.

One day they were mixing a white chemical that looked like sugar. Neil walked in and asked what they were doing. They showed him the chemical they were mixing. When he asked what the chemical was, Kotcho told him it was $C_{12}H_{22}O_{11}$, which he had just learned was the chemical definition of sugar. He thought Neil wouldn't know that meant "sugar."

Neil also knew the chemical term. He thought it was sugar and put a handful in his mouth. He immediately spit it out. It tasted awful! Kotcho and Bud felt terrible. They were afraid they had poisoned him!

"Are you all right?" Bud asked.

"Yeah, I'm okay," Neil replied. "But it sure tasted awful."

Neil went home to work on his project for the science fair. He had decided to make a little steam turbine out of wood. Cutting the wood and gluing the pieces together, he put a wooden frame together. Then he made a little wheel. He found a small pan in which he could put water. Then he placed a candle under the pan to heat the water.

As he was working, his little brother, Dean, kept asking questions. "Why do you have a candle?"

"I'm going to light it and heat the water in this little pan."

"Why?"

"It will make the water so hot that it will turn to steam."

Mrs. Armstrong watched Neil build his steam turbine. She was pleased that he was so creative. And her eyes twinkled as she listened to all of Dean's questions. He was learning just the way Neil had.

Neil was just about to light the candle when the doorbell rang. Mrs. Armstrong opened the door and Kotcho was there.

"Is Neil all right?" he asked in a worried tone.

"Why?" Neil's mother asked. Her eyebrows lifted in a questioning way. "Come on in. He's working on his project for the science fair."

"I'm in the kitchen," Neil called.

Kotcho felt relieved when he saw Neil working. He was glad that Neil was okay.

He looked at what Neil was building. He felt a little envious. The steam turbine engine looked like a neat project, maybe better than Bud's and his project.

As it turned out, it was better than the photoelectric cell. When Bud and Kotcho had completed their project and were testing it, they could not get the photoelectric cell to work! They tried shining all kinds of lights on the cell. Nothing worked!

The day before the science fair, Bud and Kotcho knew they had to do something different. So at the last minute they made a pinhole camera. They used an oatmeal box and covered it with wet tissue paper. They punched a tiny hole in the front of the box, which was the opening of the camera. They then placed film in the homemade camera and took several pictures. After they took the pictures, they developed them in a darkroom in the basement.

At the science fair the boys were assigned to set up their projects next to each other. When Neil saw the fuzzy pictures, he laughed.

"Where is your photoelectric cell?" he asked them.

"We couldn't get it to work," Bud replied.

"When did you make this camera?" Neil asked.

"Yesterday . . . we had to do something."

Neil didn't respond, but he felt like saying that the poor project looked like it had been thrown together yesterday. He then set up his little steam turbine, which worked perfectly.

The visitors to the science fair walked up and down past the tables to look at all of the students' projects. There were parents, teachers, and other students admiring the many different science demonstrations.

Neil lit the candle, and soon the water in the pan was boiling. The steam rose, and the little wheel went round and round. Many people stopped to watch his project.

When all the water had boiled away, he refilled the pan and heated the water again. And again the little wheel went round and round. Neil spent nearly all morning showing how his steam engine turbine worked. Finally it came time for the judges to view the projects.

The judges were three science teachers. Slowly they walked up and down the aisles, looking carefully at each project and taking notes.

Neil had filled his little bowl with water, heated it almost to boiling, and then blown out the candle to wait for the judges before relighting it. He watched when the judges stopped to look at Bud and Kotcho's pinhole camera. He lit the candle and watched as the steam began to form. The judges looked carefully at the pictures that the boys had taken with the camera. Then they moved over to see Neil's project.

The steam rose, but the little wheel didn't turn. The judges waited patiently. The steam was thick and poured up through the little wheel. But it didn't budge. Neil wanted to give it a push-start with his hand, but he knew he couldn't do that. After waiting a short time and asking questions about the steam turbine, the judges moved on.

Neil looked over his project until he discovered why it would not work. He had run it so much that the wood surrounding the wheel had swollen from the moisture. The wheel no longer had enough room to turn. He removed the water and burned the candle low so that the wood would dry out. Finally, at the very end of the judging, the wood dried enough that he was able to get the wheel to turn with the steam.

He asked if the judges would come back and look at his project once again, but they wouldn't. The three friends were all surprised when Kotcho and Bud got a first

prize of "Superior" on their very simple project, which they had put together at the last minute, and Neil got only a "Good" for his project!

At the end of the summer after ninth grade, the Armstrong family moved to Wapakoneta, Ohio. At one time they had lived in St. Marys, which is very close to Wapakoneta, and needed to decide to which town they would move. It is said that Neil's parents decided on Wapakoneta because Blume High School had a very fine science and math program. They wanted him to be able to continue his work in high school science. It turned out to be a very wise decision.

Another New School

In 1944, NEIL and his family moved to Wapakoneta. Neil was entering his sophomore year in high school. That same year, Grover Crites, a science and math teacher, came to Blume High School.

The first day of school, Neil walked the three blocks from his new home. Other boys and girls were walking along to school also.

Although Neil was sorry to leave his friends in Upper Sandusky, he felt at home in Wapakoneta. His grandparents' farm was only six miles from town, and he had visited there all his life. The family had moved into a comfortable house, and Neil's room was already filled with the model airplanes he had built.

The boys and girls at Blume High School were very friendly, and Neil's classes were interesting. Blume had only about four hundred students, so it wasn't long before Neil knew just about everybody in the whole school. He played the baritone horn in the school band and joined the boys' club and many other activities.

Neil's father became the Scoutmaster of the local Boy Scout troop, and Neil was once again very active in the Scouts. Like his old Wolf Patrol, his new patrol met weekly so the boys could work on their merit badges. Now their goal was to become Eagle Scouts.

Neil and the other boys studied the solar system to earn their astronomy badge. The whole patrol visited a small homemade observatory where they talked with Jacob Zint, the man who had built it.

The night was clear and cold as the group of boys walked down to Mr. Zint's house on West Auglaize Street. There was a light dusting of snow on the ground, and the dark sky was lit by the full Moon.

Jacob Zint had built his observatory on top of his garage. He had fairly good equipment, and he enjoyed talking to people about the solar system.

This evening he explained to the boys all about the stars and the planets. The boys had read in their Scout handbook that Earth and all the other heavenly bodies were part of one big family belonging to the Sun.

"Because the Moon is full tonight and so bright, it is difficult to see all the stars in the sky," Mr. Zint explained to them. He told them that the Moon orbits Earth and that it reflects the light of the Sun.

"Plan to come back in a couple of weeks or so," Mr. Zint said, "when the sky is darker and we can get a better look at all the stars."

The Scout patrol went to Jacob Zint's observatory often to learn about the stars. Even after they had completed the work for their merit badges, they continued to go to his observatory to talk with him.

Most of the boys in Wapakoneta had jobs, and Neil was no different. He worked for a while at the West End Market as a stock boy, then at Bowsher's Hardware, and then at Rhine and Brading's Pharmacy. He swept out the drugstore in the morning before school and went back after school to clerk. He also worked on Saturdays stocking shelves, working the cash register, and doing anything else they asked him to do. He was paid forty cents an hour.

Neil made many friends in Wapakoneta. In school, students presented programs during school assemblies. So Neil and his new friends Bob Gustafson, Jerre Maxson, and Jim Mougey decided to form a jazz combo to perform at an assembly.

Neil saved his money to buy a baritone horn. With Neil on horn, Jerre Maxson and Bob Gustafson both on trombone, and Jim Mougey on clarinet, they started their four-man jazz group. They got together often to practice and called themselves the Mississippi Moonshiners.

Their high school friends really liked their music. What they lacked in ability, they made up for in pep and enthusiasm.

But Neil's life centered around airplanes. He wanted to become a pilot someday, and an aeronautical engineer, a person who builds planes. To reach his goals, Neil knew he had to learn everything he could about the universe.

He often stayed after school to work in the science lab with his teacher, Mr. Crites. Together they talked about how the world worked. It was Neil's first step to realizing his dreams.

At a parent-teacher conference, Mr. and Mrs. Armstrong met with Mr. Crites. He told them Neil was an exceptional student with high goals. He said Neil should go to a university to prepare for a career.

"Neil wants to do something daring and different," Mr. Crites told Mr. and Mrs. Armstrong.

Neil's parents were very pleased with Neil's progress and that he wanted to go to college. They were also glad that he had such a great teacher to help him reach his goals.

But they were also worried. They knew how much a college education would cost for each of their three children.

Viola sighed, "I know we will manage, but I don't quite see how we will be able to afford college for Neil, Dean, and June."

"It is important that they all go to college. It'll work out. . . ." Stephen replied.

"Well, Neil is saving a little money from his job for college. We will just have to find a way to save a little, too, so we can help him."

Mrs. Armstrong was concerned. She knew

116

that they would do it, but she didn't quite see how.

The spring of 1945 brought dramatic changes to the United States. President Franklin Delano Roosevelt died suddenly, and Harry S. Truman became president. In May of 1945, the war in Europe ended with the Allies victorious. On May 8, Wapakoneta, along with the entire rest of the country, celebrated VE Day!

There was great rejoicing again on August 14. Everyone celebrated when the war in the Pacific finally came to an end. The churches in Wapakoneta held special services. Church bells rang, horns honked, and fireworks were set off in jubilation. Finally, after almost four years, the world was at peace again.

Flying Lessons

NEIL SPENT AS much time as he could at the Port Koneta Airport, three or four miles out of town on Old Brewery Road. When he could, he would hitchhike out to look at all the planes. Sometimes he would even earn a little money washing down a plane.

He knew he had to learn to fly, so he talked to his mother and father about taking flying lessons.

"How much do flying lessons cost?" his father asked.

"Nine dollars an hour," Neil answered quietly.

"And how much do you make an hour at Rhine and Brading's Pharmacy?"

"Forty cents," he replied.

"You have our permission to take the lessons, but they are too expensive for us to pay for. You will have to pay for them, which means you'll have to work many hours to pay for just one hour."

Neil nodded. He knew it would take a long time before he could get enough money to get the hours for a pilot's license.

"It's going to take a long time, but it's what I want to do. I want to be a pilot, so I'll save my money for lessons."

Neil was fifteen years old when he first started taking lessons from Aubrey Knudegard in an Aeronca Champion.

Whenever he had enough money and a day off from work, he went out to the airport for lessons. Sometimes he went for lessons on Sunday mornings before church. When he did, though, he made sure that he

had enough time to get back before church started.

Neil often had to hitch a ride or walk to the airport. In this small town, it usually wasn't too much trouble to get a ride from someone going in that direction.

One afternoon, the ladies at the St. Paul's Evangelical and Reformed Church were preparing supper at the church. Mrs. Armstrong, who always could be counted on to help, was working in the kitchen. One of the ladies who was working with her said, "My husband gave Neil a ride to the airport on Saturday."

"That was good of him," Mrs. Armstrong replied as she continued scrubbing the vegetables for the salad.

"Al said that Neil is taking flying lessons."

Neil's mother smiled. She knew that Mary Sue was trying to find out what Neil was doing. "That's right. He is learning how to fly," she answered calmly.

Mary Sue's eyes widened. "Aren't you worried about his safety?" she exclaimed.

"Of course I want Neil to be safe. But learning to fly is very important to him. He has very good judgment and I am sure he will be careful."

Stephen and Viola Armstong were very proud of Neil when he got his student pilot's license on August 5, 1946, his sixteenth birthday. But he still had to ride his bike wherever he went in Wapakoneta, because he didn't have a driver's license yet!

Neil's father understood Neil's fascination with flying. And though his mother was also proud of his accomplishments in flying, she did worry a little about it, and with good reason.

One late afternoon when Neil was riding home from Boy Scout camp with his father, they came upon a terrible accident. An airplane had crashed! Then they heard that the young pilot, a fellow student of Neil's, had died in the crash.

When Neil and his father reached their house, Neil went straight up to his room without a word. Mrs. Armstrong looked at her husband. "What's wrong with Neil?"

"We were driving down the road from Scout camp when we saw a number of people and cars around an accident in the field. I thought there must have been a car crash . . . but the accident was so far off the road. When we came closer we could see that a small plane had gone down."

"Oh, my! And the pilot? Was he all right?" Neil's mother asked fearfully.

Stephen Armstrong took a deep breath. "He was killed. Neil knew him."

Neil spent most of the next two days in his room. He didn't talk about the accident, but he didn't give up flying, either.

Neil studied diligently in school and he worked hard at his job at the drugstore trying to save money for college as well as flying lessons. He heard about college scholarships that the navy offered. Neil was not really interested in a career in the navy, but he sent in an application. He knew it wouldn't hurt to apply. If he received one of those scholarships, it would certainly help!

Neil wanted to study aeronautical engineering, but he realized that would require a strong math and science background. Luckily, Mr. Crites was a very dedicated teacher. He was willing to work with Neil and all his students outside of class to help them.

In the spring of Neil's senior year, the letter arrived that he had received a U.S. Navy scholarship to the university of his choice. He had almost forgotten about sending in the application and certainly wasn't expecting this wonderful news! It was 1947, and Neil was only sixteen years old.

Waving the letter in his hand, Neil called loudly, "Mom! Mom!"

His mother was down in the basement getting out quart jars of canned fruit to bake some pies. His loud calls frightened her. She was so startled that she dropped a jar of blackberries on her big toe!

Neil came bounding down the stairs, shouting in delight, "I got the scholarship, Mom! I got the scholarship!"

Mrs. Armstrong had slid down to sit on the floor. She pulled her injured foot back from the broken glass and the puddle of blackberries in their juice. "What do you mean? What scholarship?"

Neil knelt down by his mother to show her the letter. He explained to her that he had received a U.S. Navy scholarship that would pay for his college expenses!

Mrs. Armstrong was delighted, as was the rest of the family when they heard the news.

Mrs. Armstrong limped on her bruised, broken toe for weeks, but she didn't complain about it. It only reminded her of the wonderful news that Neil was going to college on a scholarship!

Airplanes to
Astronauts

NEIL AND HIS parents talked about where he
should go to college.

Mr. Armstrong's face was serious as he
studied the various college catalogs. "It's
important to get the best education you can,
and with this scholarship you have that
opportunity."

Neil thought about going to the Massa-
chusetts Institute of Technology, but his high
school teachers suggested that he go to
Purdue University. It had a strong aeronautical engineering school.

When he talked about it with his parents, they agreed that Purdue seemed the best choice. Not only did it have a highly respected program, but Purdue University was in Lafayette, Indiana, not very far from home. Mrs. Armstrong didn't say anything, but, to her, Neil seemed too young to be leaving home for college. She would be happier if he were not too far away.

The first few days at Purdue University were exciting, but the school was so large. As he walked through the campus with all its enormous redbrick buildings, he looked in amazement at the hundreds of students hurrying along in all directions.

Neil entered the aeronautical engineering program. The classes were difficult, but he was learning things that he wanted to know.

He played baritone horn in the band and soon made friends. He was very surprised to see that Bud Blackford, his friend from Upper Sandusky, was also in the band.

Neil enjoyed being at Purdue, but he only got to stay there for a short time. After only a year and a half, the navy called him into active duty.

At nineteen years old, Neil was ordered to Pensacola, Florida, for flight training. He chose to train in single-engine fighters. Neil received his wings shortly after the Korean War broke out on June 25, 1950. He was only twenty years old when he was assigned to Fighter Squadron 51. This squadron was one of the earliest all-jet carrier squadrons to be sent into action.

After Neil received his wings, he had a short leave at home in Wapakoneta before he was sent with his squadron to Korea. June and Dean were glad to have their big brother home. They asked him all about flight school and Florida. It was exciting to think about Neil going off to Korea and flying airplanes off the deck of a carrier!

Mother made all of Neil's favorite foods.

She baked pies and cakes. And she laughed as she said, "No blackberry pies, Neil! All the blackberries landed on my toe and on the basement floor!"

Grandmother Korspeter was delighted to spend time with Neil. She was always very cheerful. She thought, though, about her father who had left Germany and come to this country to get away from the wars. And now Neil was going off to fight in one.

His family was worried, but they knew that he was a good pilot, and they would pray for his safety. As he left, his father gave him a strong pat on the back. His mother kissed him quickly and gave him a care package of food, including a supply of her good cookies.

At twenty, Neil Armstrong was one of the youngest pilots in his squadron. He flew Panther jets on seventy-eight combat missions off the carrier *Essex* during the Korean War. The squadron had been trained for air-

to-air combat, but there were no enemy planes in their area. Their work was to damage bridges, stop trains, and shoot tanks and other targets. This meant they had to fly at very low altitudes, which was very dangerous. Many of the pilots in this squadron were killed or injured.

Armstrong received three air medals for his outstanding service during the Korean War. Once he nursed a badly damaged jet back to the deck of the *Essex*. Another time, very low to the ground, he clipped a wing on a cable that stretched across a North Korean valley. He was able to fly the plane far enough into friendly territory, then parachute out safely. He was a very brave pilot.

After the Korean War, in the fall of 1952, he returned to Purdue University to continue his college education and earn his degree in aeronautical engineering. After his navy service, Neil was more mature and experienced as he returned to school. He studied very hard, but he also enjoyed spending time with friends. He joined a fraternity and was a member of the American Rocket Society. He was president of the Aero Club and a member of the Institute of Aeronautical Sciences.

Early in the morning when he was delivering the campus newspaper on the Purdue campus, he often met a pretty, dark-haired girl, whose name was Janet Shearon, as she was going to her classes. She was a home economics major and had some six A.M. laboratory courses.

Jan had some interest in airplanes, also. Her father, who was a physician in the Chicago area, had a plane to go to and from the family's summer home in Wisconsin. Her mother and her two older sisters had all taken flight instruction. Neil and Jan enjoyed talking with each other and became friends. They started dating after Neil graduated in January 1955.

After Neil's graduation, and as he looked for job opportunities, he noticed that the National Advisory Committee on Aeronautics, which later became known as the National Aeronautics and Space Administration, or NASA, was doing some interesting things. He applied for a job at Edwards Air Force Base in California; however, there weren't any jobs open. Then he received a call from the Lewis Flight Propulsion Laboratory for a job in Cleveland. He worked there in a free-flight rocket group and later with the pilot group. Neil told Abe Silverstein, the associate director of Lewis Laboratory, that he thought space travel was going to become a reality and that he would like to be a part of it.

In 1955, space travel was not taken seriously, but Neil felt Edwards Air Force Base was the place to be. And then suddenly it had a job opening! Neil received a call asking him if he would be interested in coming to Edwards. Interested! He was delighted, and accepted immediately!

On his way driving to southern California from Cleveland, he went out of his way to drive to northern Wisconsin, where Janet

Shearon was working as a camp counselor. He asked her to marry him and go with him to California. She said yes, but they weren't married until January of 1956, and then she joined him.

Those early days in 1955 and 1956 at Edwards Air Force Base were wonderful. Neil Armstrong was doing exactly what he wanted to do.

After Neil and Jan were married, instead of taking a house in Lancaster, California, the nearby town, like most of the other test pilots, they got a former forest ranger's cabin far up in the San Gabriel Mountains. The house was very simple. It didn't even have hot water.

Neil had the most exciting time of his life at Edwards Air Force Base. As a research pilot, he flew almost every kind of high-performance airplane. He flew over two hundred different models of aircraft, including jets, rockets, helicopters, and gliders! At the same time, he was doing research in aerodynamics. He flew the X-15 for the first time in 1960. He flew the X-15 a total of seven times, 4,000 miles an hour, to an altitude of 207,000 feet! The X-15 was a rocket-propelled research aircraft that flew higher and faster than any other airplane in history. It was designed to bridge the gap between flying in the atmosphere and flight in space.

The flight took only about ten minutes, but Neil needed to get a lot of information while he was in flight. Flying above 200,000 feet gives the same type of view as you would have from a spacecraft when you are above the atmosphere. And what a view it was! Neil could see the curvature of the earth!

The X-15 was launched in the air from a special Boeing B-52. From the Armstrongs' house far up in the mountains, through her binoculars, Jan could see the X-15 aircraft drop away from the B-52 mother airship and go into flight. And on its return she could see the dust rise down in the valley as the X-15 landed on the twenty-five-mile-long dry lake bed at Edwards.

Neil's work at Edwards was in flight research. They searched for answers to the problems of flight. They were not just pilots. They worked as engineers and planners. Armstrong said, "We were using airplanes as tools to gather all kinds of information, just as an astronomer uses a telescope as a tool. We didn't fly often, but when we did, it was unbelievably exciting."

They even worked on some of the problems for the Mercury astronauts. At Edwards they made a capsule, which was about the same weight as the Mercury spacecraft, and dropped it again and again from 70,000 feet. They were trying to test the parachute at about the same height and speed as it was needed for the Mercury.

At this time, Neil felt that he was doing

more for space flight research than the Mercury astronauts were. Later, he changed his mind.

Successes and
Failures

ARMSTRONG WAS A natural to become an astronaut. At Edwards Air Force Base, he had been chosen to fly an aircraft in the Dyna-Soar project. This aircraft was to be part spacecraft and part airplane. When it looked as if the Dyna-Soar aircraft was going to be canceled, he applied for the astronaut program.

Neil Armstrong became the first civilian to become an astronaut. On September 17, 1962, he was accepted into NASA's second astronaut class, known as "The Nine" to differentiate them from the first group, known as the "Original Seven."

Armstrong was named to the backup crew for Gemini 5, whose crew were Gordon Cooper and Charles "Pete" Conrad. But it was in Gemini 8, as command pilot, with David Scott as copilot, that he first went up in the spacecraft. As the flight turned out, it was extremely fortunate that he was an excellent pilot with his years of experience in manually controlling his aircraft.

On March 16, 1966, the Gemini 8 was launched with the goal of docking with another orbiting vehicle, an unmanned Agena target satellite. In order to dock, the spacecraft needed to catch up with the satellite. Commander Neil Armstrong would have to position the spacecraft in order to meet the satellite. Then Armstrong and Scott would join the two craft together in midspace. David Scott was scheduled to make a space walk, which could last as long as one orbit of the earth. The flight was expected to last two days. The docking took place successfully, but Scott did not have the opportunity to make his space walk.

The twenty-seven-foot long *Agena* lifted from pad 14 at ten A.M., and in only a few minutes settled into a 298 kilometer circular orbit. Fourteen minutes before the Atlas rocket blasted the *Agena* into space, Neil Armstrong and David Scott slipped through the hatches into their couches on the spacecraft. When they were told of the *Agena*'s nearly perfect orbit, Neil Armstrong said, "Beautiful, we will take that one."

At 10:40 A.M., the *Gemini* spacecraft was sent aloft by the powerful *Titan 2* rocket. The *Agena* had a 1,963-kilometer head start when Armstrong and Scott began to try to catch up with the target satellite.

The Sun set a half hour or so into their flight. As they sped along, they had time to sightsee. They could see some of the islands of Hawaii. And then only minutes later they saw Los Angeles, California.

Over the Pacific Ocean, twenty-five minutes before completing the second orbit, Armstrong adjusted the thrusters to push the spacecraft into the orbit of the *Agena*. Next Armstrong and Scott were able to locate the target with their radar. Nearly an hour later they saw the target *Agena* gleaming in the sunshine. Armstrong piloted the spacecraft skillfully, with Scott telling him the exact amount and direction of thrust they needed.

They felt a solid contact as they closed the final few inches and latched the two vehicles together. There was a soft thump in the cockpit when the *Agena* docked, but outside in space there was only silence. Armstrong exclaimed with gusto, "Flight, we are docked! . . . It's really a smoothie." The docking was one hundred percent manually flown, and it was good to hear Neil

Armstrong say it was easy. The flight controllers in Houston were delighted. This was the first successful docking of two vehicles in space! This was important because it was a necessary step to learn before they could send men to the Moon.

Armstrong and Scott flew the ship for about thirty minutes. The *Gemini 8* was supposed to be flying level, but David Scott noticed on the control panel that they had a 30-degree roll. He frowned as he said, "Neil, we're in a bank."

Neil managed to stop the motion for a short time, but it started again. They thought it was the *Agena* that was causing the trouble. Scott turned off the target's control system. For four minutes the two craft straightened up, and the problem seemed to be over. Armstrong started to try to get the *Gemini* spacecraft with its docked *Agena* into the correct position. And suddenly they began to roll again, faster and faster!

Armstrong struggled with the controls. Scott turned the switches of the *Agena* off and on and off. Then Armstrong turned the spacecraft switches off and on. They tried to find the problem. Nothing they did helped.

They decided that they would have to separate from the *Agena*. Scott hit the undocking button. Armstrong gave the thrusters a long hard burst, and the spacecraft backed off immediately.

Almost at once Armstrong and Scott knew that the trouble was with the spacecraft as the *Gemini* rolled faster and faster. "Then we really took off," Armstrong said later.

"We have serious problems here . . . we're tumbling end over end up here," Scott reported. "We have separated from the *Agena*."

"We're rolling up and we can't turn anything off. Continuously increasing in a left roll," Armstrong said.

After backing away from the *Agena*, the

spacecraft started to spin at a dizzying rate. Armstrong's and Scott's vision was blurred.

"All that we've got left is the reentry control system," said Armstrong. They tried to get into the reentry control system, but were not able to. Finally the hand controllers worked!

Armstrong was able to steady the motion, and he could tell that it was the number 8 thruster that had stuck open. Using the reentry control thrusters meant that the *Gemini 8*'s mission would have to end as soon as possible.

The chief flight director had only one choice to make. That would be where the *Gemini* should come down. The recommendation of the Landing and Recovery Division was to go for a touchdown in the Pacific Ocean in the seventh orbit.

Meanwhile, the navy in the Pacific was steaming into action. The destroyer USS *Leonard F. Mason* sped toward the expected

147

landing point east of Okinawa, Japan. Armstrong was concerned that they might come down in some remote wilderness where they would be hard to find.

Everything went well during their descent. As they approached Earth's surface, Armstrong asked Scott, "Do you see water out there?"

"All I see is a haze," Scott replied, and then with joy he exclaimed, "Oh, yes, there's water! It's water!" Two minutes later, he yelled, *Landing—safe.*"

They had splashed down into the Pacific Ocean after 6.5 Earth orbits, 10.7 hours of flight, far short of the goals of the mission's flight plan.

An HC-54 Rescuemaster from the Naha Air Base in Okinawa reached the spacecraft with three para-rescuemen ready to jump. Armstrong and Scott saw one of the three as he parachuted down. The frogmen had trouble securing the flotation collar to the spacecraft because of the rough seas. They continued to work at it and had the collar on the spacecraft within forty-five minutes of the landing.

Three hours later, the USS *Mason* pulled alongside and fastened a line to the spacecraft. With the rough sea, climbing the Jacob's ladder was hard, but they did it. On deck Armstrong and Scott managed smiles for the welcoming sailors. But still having upset stomachs from the dizzy ride and the high waves, they went straight to the sick bay.

The USS *Mason* reached Okinawa the next day, where they received a hero's welcome. They then flew on to Hawaii and home.

Neil Armstrong felt sorry that the flight had to be cut short. But they had had no other choice. Armstrong and Scott were both very disappointed that David Scott was not able to make his two-hour walk in space. Scott had spent months in training for a very involved space walk using new chestpacks and backpacks. Now he would never be able to find out how the equipment would have worked, or how it would feel to float in space.

It was said that Neil Armstrong's skill in bringing the spacecraft safely back to Earth made "a very great impression" on the NASA officials who selected the crews for the first Moon landing missions.

Armstrong was honored at Purdue University in May of 1966 after the *Gemini 8* flight. He presented to Dr. Hovde, the president of Purdue, the black and gold Purdue flag that he had taken with him on the *Gemini* flight. He said, "I carried this flag in honor of those many Purdue individuals in industry, in government service, and in the education community who have been so deeply involved in our program, and for all of you who would like to have ridden with me in fact and did ride with me in spirit."

In accepting the flag, Dr. Hovde spoke of his pride in the Purdue men in the astronaut program, and that he was sure when the *Apollo* would make its landing on the Moon there would be a Purdue man aboard.

Of course, Neil Armstrong would be that man, but he had yet another close call—nearly losing his life—before he had the chance to go to the Moon.

At Ellington Air Force Base on May 6, 1968, Armstrong was practicing in a free-flight trainer known as the Lunar Landing Research Vehicle (LLRV), nicknamed "the Flying Bedstead." The vehicle was a jet-and-rocket-powered craft without wings. It had a single-seat, box-shaped cockpit, a tail section, and four spindly landing legs. Because of the vehicle's awkward body, and because he was flying it in Earth's gravity instead of the one-sixth gravity of the Moon, handling the LLRV was far more difficult than working with a real lunar module on the Moon. It was also more dangerous.

Neil Armstrong was in the final stage of his

landing. He was less than two hundred feet from the ground when the LLRV suddenly began spinning and backfiring. A thick cloud of engine exhaust poured out. Then suddenly the vehicle pitched nose up, rolled over to the right, and tumbled toward the ground. After a few breathless seconds of trying to right the craft, he finally hit the ejection handle. Armstrong parachuted onto a patch of grass between the runways. The LLRV slammed into the pavement and burst into flames. Neil Armstrong picked himself up and walked to the hangar as he looked back at the burning wreck.

Preparations

THE NAMES OF the crew for the *Apollo 11* were announced on January 9, 1969. They were Neil Armstrong, Edwin "Buzz" Aldrin, and Mike Collins. The three had worked together for over a year. They were the team of backup pilots for the *Apollo 8* mission. They had studied the *Saturn 5* rocket. They had worked in ground training to learn all about it. The *Saturn 5* was the rocket that blasted the *Apollo 8* into flight. They learned about the *Apollo 8* command module and its flight to the Moon. And finally they studied the reentry of the fiery command module to splashdown. The *Apollo 8* had just completed its mission. The *Apollo 11* was scheduled to be the first Moon-landing flight.

The Apollo flights going before the *Apollo 11* would need to complete their missions before the Moon landing would be possible. These flights would need to complete many exercises to perfect the ways the two modules would connect and separate. They also would have to prove the reliability of the spiderlike Moon-landing module, the lunar module. If the lunar module did not work well, the landing on the Moon might be delayed until the *Apollo 12* flight. On the other hand, if the preparations were ahead of schedule, the Moon landing might even be set up for the *Apollo 10* flight. So in January of 1969, it was not absolutely sure that Neil Armstrong, Mike Collins, and Buzz Aldrin would be the first Moon-landing crew.

Never was there a more complete preparation for a mission. Men and women and their computers had worked for years on the mathematics of the equipment, the course of the flight, and the risks. Thousands of people had worked on every detail, and hundreds of manufacturers produced the equipment, which had been built to the most careful and precise specifications. The massive *Saturn 5* rocket, the *Apollo 11* spaceship, and the Moon-landing module were tested in every possible way, both on the ground and in space. The elaborate preparations continued right up until the launch.

From January to the July 16 date of the launch, Neil Armstrong, Mike Collins, and Buzz Aldrin were busy preparing. Neil Armstrong, commander of the mission, and the crew studied long hours learning their mission plan. For nearly half of their training time they practiced operating the guidance and navigation computer. Hours were spent

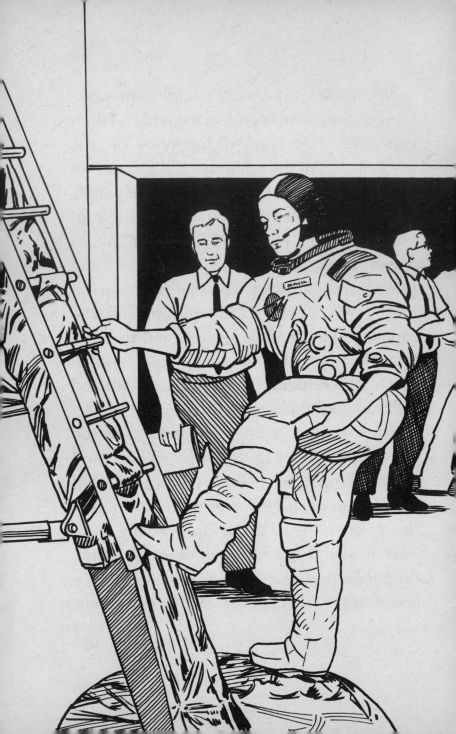

in the centrifuge in Houston. This was never a pleasant experience, and when it was imitating returns from the Moon, it was especially bad. They worked in a large vacuum chamber and gained experience in weightlessness during sudden dips in a KC-135 airplane.

The NASA Center at Langley, Virginia, had full-scale replicas of the command module and the lunar module. The astronauts had to inspect them and simulate flying them. They tried to think of what kinds of problems there might be when the two real modules docked in space.

Mike Collins trained long hours in the command module simulator. Neil and Buzz also trained for hours and hours in the lunar module and on their lunar surface training. Then there were many hours in which Neil, Buzz, and Mike trained together as a unit. Each of the men spent over four hundred hours working in simulators.

There were many decisions that needed to be made. For one, they needed to think up a name for the spacecraft, and also to design an emblem for the mission. Several of the group talked about what the emblem should be. Jim Lovell mentioned an American eagle. Mike Collins looked up a book on birds where he found a perfect picture of a bald eagle coming in for a landing. And so the mission emblem was designed with an eagle holding an olive branch in his feet, a symbol of a peaceful expedition.

The eagle on the mission emblem made the naming of the landing craft the *Eagle* a natural. It took a little more time to come up with a name for the command module. The *Columbia* was suggested by Julian Scheer, of NASA's public affairs office in Washington, D.C. Mike Collins said that he kept thinking about the song "Columbia, the Gem of the Ocean," and that seemed to be a suitable name for the spacecraft that would land in the ocean. Neil Armstrong and Buzz Aldrin agreed, so the *Columbia* it was!

Armstrong and Aldrin, who would actually walk on the Moon, spent hours learning geology and photography. On the Moon's surface they would be taking pictures, and throughout the mission there would be telecasts back to Earth. They studied maps of the Moon. They also worked on the problem of walking on the surface of the Moon. Man's weight on the Moon would be just one-sixth of his weight on Earth, but his size would remain the same.

There were two ways they could simulate a walk on the Moon. One was to use an airplane flying a trajectory similar to no gravity. For thirty-second periods a man could walk under one-sixth gravity. Another way was a "Peter Pan rig." The man stood straight as he was held up by a cable-and-pulley system weighted with five-sixths of the man's weight. "You had the feeling of being able to jump very high . . . a very light feeling," said Neil Armstrong. "It was a sort of floating sensation." Perhaps it felt a little like his childhood dream of floating.

After four months of very difficult training, Armstrong, Aldrin, and Collins were very tired. They had been spending up to fourteen hours a day in their simulators, enormous machines that one man called "the great train wreck." The command module simulator was an enormous, gaudy machine, with a carpeted staircase up to the cockpit entrance some fifteen feet above the door. The cockpit was an exact model of an Apollo command module cockpit, with all the controls, switches, dials, gauges, and computer display panels. It was surrounded on all sides by huge boxes placed at peculiar angles. On these boxes were images similar to what the pilot would see out the windows. The computer was in a glass case all by itself, with its own large crew.

With Armstrong and Aldrin in the lunar module simulator and the people at mission control at their computers, they would practice all the real situations the crew might experience on their trip to the Moon. The astronauts spent all week in those simulators at Cape Kennedy in Florida and would fly back to Houston every weekend.

In addition, Neil Armstrong, as flight commander, had to fly the lunar landing training vehicle, "the Flying Bedstead," a machine similar to the one in which he had almost lost his life.

Neil's wife, Jan, said that she was worried about them all. "The worst time was in early June. They were discouraged. They worried about whether there was time enough for them to learn the things they needed to learn, to do the things they had to do. . . ."

That changed when the decision was made for the launch date to go forward on July 16, 1969. When the astronauts knew they were really going, everything got better. They knew they would be ready.

On June 27, the dress rehearsal, called the Countdown Demonstration Test for *Apollo 11*, began. All the steps of the actual countdown, the checks, the fueling of the rocket, and the entrance of the astronauts into the spacecraft cabin were included. On July 3, just before 9:32 A.M., came the instruction, "You're cleared for firing command," through the intercom at Firing Room 1. A few seconds later, a man pressed the button that began the automatic three-minute, seven-second sequence of computerized events leading to liftoff. The countdown ticked away to the point of ignition. But at that point it stopped. It was only make-believe. A final practice.

The astronauts practiced the first twelve minutes of the flight again and again. The instructors operated the computers that ran the simulator. Sometimes the pretend liftoff was perfect. Other times the instructors put in an error or two to test the astronauts' knowledge and quickness of thinking.

On July 10, 1969, at 8:00 P.M., the master clock in Firing Room 1 began ticking. It was the beginning of the real countdown. Launching controllers began sending electric power to the tall, silent *Saturn 5* rocket that was ready and waiting.

At their last press conference, two nights before the flight, a newsman asked if they had any fears about the mission. Neil Armstrong replied that of course they all had experienced fear. "But we have no fear . . . on undertaking this expedition." And then Armstrong said that after a decade of planning and hard work, "we're willing and ready to attempt to achieve our national goal" of putting a man on the Moon!

The First Man on
the Moon

ON THE MORNING of July 16, 1969, the huge, 363-foot-tall, gleaming white *Apollo 11* stood at Launch Pad 39A at Cape Kennedy. Waiting for the launch was a worldwide television audience, including the families of the crew. In Wapakoneta, Ohio, Stephen and Viola Armstrong sat in their living room. They watched and waited for the launch that would send their son into space on his way to becoming the first man to set foot on the Moon.

Also watching and waiting was Neil Armstrong's eighty-one-year-old grandmother.

Caroline Korspeter had been fifteen years old when Orville Wright had made that first historic flight at Kitty Hawk, North Carolina. Now, not quite sixty-six years later, she was watching her grandson Neil in a spacecraft, waiting to be launched to the Moon.

There were an estimated one million people at Cape Kennedy anxiously waiting for this historic launch. The hordes of people were tense with anticipation, their gaze fixed on the huge rocket. Seated in grandstands or standing on the sand flats three and one-half miles away were former President Lyndon B.

Johnson and Mrs. Johnson, half the members of the United States Congress, and more than three thousand journalists from the United States and from fifty-five other countries. On board the *Apollo 11* were astronauts Neil Armstrong, commander; Michael Collins, command module pilot; and Edwin "Buzz" Aldrin, Jr., lunar module pilot.

A flame appeared on the horizon as the first of *Saturn 5's* enormous first-stage engines ignited. Soon the other four engines fired, and the light of the first engines lit the scene like a rising sun. Moments after, at 9:32 A.M., the *Apollo 11* blasted off with brilliant orange flames and the smoke at its base rolling upward. The entire area was shattered with an enormous wave of crackling sound.

From mission control the last words were, "Good luck and Godspeed."

"Thank you very much," Commander Armstrong replied. "We know this will be a good flight."

After the launch, the first-stage engines were dropped and the second-stage engines fired. These were also dropped.

Within three minutes from liftoff, the spacecraft was 37 nautical miles high, down-range 61 nautical miles, and traveling at 9,300 feet per second, or about 6,340 miles per hour! At 9:44, with a boost from the third-stage engines, *Apollo 11* entered a 103-nautical-mile-high Earth orbit.

At 12:22 P.M., midway in its second trip around Earth, the speed of *Apollo 11* was boosted by another firing of the third-stage engine to 24,200 miles per hour, which sent the spacecraft out of Earth's orbit and on the way to the Moon!

While the spacecraft moved farther and farther from Earth, the *Eagle*, the lunar landing craft, was unpacked from its compartment. The main spaceship, the *Columbia*, then docked head to head with the *Eagle*, and they continued on their way to the

Moon. The flight continued on schedule with only one midcourse correction, which improved the course of the spacecraft and tested the engine that was to get them into and out of their orbit of the Moon.

During the flight to the Moon, the astronauts telecast pictures from the spacecraft. On the evening of July 17, the telecast showed a view of Earth from a distance of about 128,000 nautical miles, and views were shown of the inside of the *Columbia,* also. The following afternoon, one of the clearest television transmissions ever sent from space was begun, with the *Columbia* 175,000 miles from Earth and 48,000 miles from the Moon. The television viewers on Earth watched as Neil Armstrong and Buzz Aldrin slid through the thirty-inch wide tunnel between the command module and the lunar module to check it out.

Midmorning of July 19, Neil Armstrong said, "The view of the Moon . . . is really spectacular. . . . We can see the entire circumference, even though part of it is in complete shadow and part of it's in Earth-shine."

At 12:58 P.M. of July 19, mission control announced they were ready to enter their Moon orbit as they said, "You are go for lunar orbit insertion."

The spacecraft passed completely behind the Moon and for the first time was out of radio contact with Earth. The spacecraft's main rocket, a 20,500-pound thrust engine, was fired for about six minutes to slow the craft so that it could be captured by the gravity of the Moon. And then, a more even orbit around the Moon was established by another burn of the main engine for only seventeen seconds.

That evening, Armstrong and Aldrin again squeezed through the tunnel to check the lunar module. On the morning of July 20, Aldrin crawled into the lunar module and started to power up the *Eagle*. About an hour later, Armstrong joined him, and together they continued to check the systems and deploy the landing legs.

At 1:46 P.M., the Moon-landing craft, the *Eagle*, was separated from the *Columbia*, the command module. The *Columbia*, piloted by Mike Collins, continued to orbit the Moon. At 3:08 P.M., Armstrong and Aldrin, flying feetfirst and facedown, fired the landing craft's descent engine for the first time. Half an hour later, as the command ship came back into radio contact with mission control, Collins reported that "everything is going swimmingly," as he informed mission control that the *Eagle* was on its way to the Moon.

The landing did not go as they had planned, and it required Armstrong's skill and quick thinking to bring the *Eagle* to rest safely on the surface of the Moon. The site they were approaching was a crater about the size of a football field and was covered with large rocks.

Quickly, Armstrong took over the manual

control and steered the craft to a smoother spot, while Aldrin gave him the altitude readings as they were coming down.

At 4:18 P.M., the craft settled down with a slight bump almost like that of a jet landing on a runway. Neil Armstrong immediately radioed mission control: "Houston, Tranquillity Base here. The *Eagle* has landed."

Aldrin, looking out of the window of the lunar module, said, "We'll get to the details around here, but it looks like a collection of just about every variety of shapes, angularities, and granularities, every variety of rock you could find. The colors vary pretty much depending on how you are looking. There doesn't appear to be much of a general color at all; however, it looks as though some of the rocks and boulders, of which there are quite a few in the near area, are going to have some interesting colors to them."

A few moments later he told of seeing numbers of craters, some of them one hun-

dred feet across, but most of them only one to two feet in diameter. He saw ridges twenty or thirty feet high, two-foot blocks with angular edges, and a hill half a mile to a mile away.

Aldrin and Armstrong first prepared the ship for leaving the Moon, making sure that everything was ready so that they would be able to take off to return to the command spacecraft orbiting above them. When everything was in order, at Armstrong's request, mission control gave them permission to start their walk on the Moon.

The astronauts put on their lunar space suits. At 10:39 P.M., Armstrong opened the hatch and squeezed through the opening. A portable life support and communications system, which weighed eighty-four pounds on Earth but only fourteen pounds on the Moon, was strapped to his shoulders. This system provided for pressurization, oxygen requirements, and removal of carbon dioxide.

Slowly he moved down the ten-foot, nine-step ladder. On reaching the second step, he pulled a ring within easy reach, which turned on a television camera that would show him to Earth. An estimated one-fourth of the earth's population shared this historic moment through television and radio.

Neil Armstrong moved down the ladder and stopped on the last step. "I'm at the foot of the ladder. The lunar module footpads are only depressed in the surface about one or two inches. The surface appears to be very, very fine-grained; as you get close to it, it's almost like a powder."

At 10:56 P.M., Neil Armstrong made that historic step on the surface of the Moon, saying, "That's one small step for a man, one giant leap for mankind." He continued, "The surface is fine and powdery. I can pick it up loosely with my toe . . . I only go in a small fraction of an inch. Maybe an eighth of an inch, but I can see the footprints of my boots and the treads in the fine, sandy particles.

There seems to be no difficulty in moving around as we suspected. It's even perhaps easier than the simulations."

Armstrong started taking a collection of soil samples close to the landing craft with a bag on the end of a pole. He collected a small bagful of soil and stored it in a pocket on the left leg of his space suit. It was planned to do this first to make sure some of the Moon surface would be returned to Earth just in case the mission had to be cut short.

Aldrin lowered a Hasselblad still camera to Armstrong, and then he came out of the landing craft and backed down the ladder as Armstrong photographed him.

As Aldrin reached the surface, he said, "Beautiful, beautiful." Armstrong replied, "Magnificent sight down here."

Armstrong focused the television camera on a small, stainless steel plaque on one of the legs of the landing craft and read aloud: "Here men from the planet Earth first set foot on the Moon, July 1969 A.D. We came in peace for all mankind." Below the inscription were the signatures of the three *Apollo 11* crew members and the signature of Richard Nixon, the president of the United States.

The astronauts set up the first of three experiments, a solar particle detector. Then, from a leg of the spacecraft, they took a three-by-five nylon United States flag and pounded the staff of the flag into the surface of the Moon. Aldrin and Armstrong stood at attention and saluted the outstretched flag of the United States of America.

At 11:47 P.M., mission control announced, "The President of the United States is in his office now and would like to speak to you."

"That would be an honor," replied Neil Armstrong.

"Neil and Buzz . . . I am talking to you from the Oval Room at the White House. And this certainly has to be the most historic telephone call ever made. For every

American, this has to be the proudest day of our lives. And for people all over the world I am sure they, too, join with Americans in recognizing what a feat this is. Because of what you have done, the heavens have become a part of man's world. As you talk to us from the Sea of Tranquillity, it inspires us to redouble our efforts to bring peace and tranquillity to Earth. For one priceless moment, in the whole history of man, all the people on this Earth are truly one."

"Thank you, Mr. President," Armstrong replied. "It's a great honor and privilege for us to be here representing not only the United States, but men of peace of all nations."

Aldrin and Armstrong then set about completing the other tasks of the mission. Armstrong used tongs and the lunar scoop to pick up a quantity of rocks and soil and seal them in boxes to take back in the landing craft. At the same time, Aldrin was setting up a seismic detector to record moonquakes and meteorite impacts or volcanic eruptions, and a laser-reflector, designed to take a more precise measurement of Earth-Moon distances.

After checking with mission control that all their chores had been completed, Aldrin started back up the ladder to reenter the lunar module. Shortly after, Armstrong, too, entered the landing craft. At 1:11 A.M., the hatch was closed. Two men from Earth had walked on the Moon for a little over two hours.

A Hero's Welcome Home

Buzz Aldrin had left the surface of the Moon and gone back into the lunar module at 12:54 A.M. on July 21. Neil Armstrong followed him in, and the hatch was closed at 1:11 A.M. A little over twelve hours later, they left the Moon at 1:54 P.M. The lunar module split in two, with the descent stage serving as the launchpad for the upper portion as they made their ascent from the Moon to meet the *Columbia*.

After four maneuvers of coming together, the *Columbia* and the *Eagle* prepared to

dock on the far side of the Moon. After the two came together and the docking latches were snapped shut, Collins threw a switch to pull the docking probe. Suddenly, the joined craft began to pitch and turn, but Collins and Armstrong used the thrusters on both vehicles and quickly regained control.

Then the lunar module was released, and shortly after midnight, the *Apollo 11* began its return from the Moon. The return to Earth took about sixty hours. The command module splashed down 825 miles southwest of Honolulu at 12:51 P.M., Thursday, July 24. It floated down into the Pacific Ocean with its three parachutes. The *Columbia's* flight to the Moon and back to Earth had taken a little over eight days and had covered 1,096,367 miles!

Collins, Aldrin, and Armstrong were taken by helicopter to the aircraft carrier USS *Hornet*, where they went into a trailerlike room to guard against the possibility of bringing any germs back from the Moon. As it turned out, there were no germs to worry about, but NASA had to be sure.

President Richard Nixon had flown many hours and thousands of miles to be aboard the USS *Hornet* to greet the astronauts. He stood on the deck of the aircraft carrier and spoke by microphone to the crew of the *Columbia*, who looked at him through the window of their quarantine trailer. As the president welcomed them back to Earth, he said, "This is the greatest week in the history of the world since the Creation."

They were returned in their trailer by a jet cargo airplane and then by a flatbed truck to Houston. The three men remained in quarantine until Sunday, August 10, 1969, when it was announced they were all in good physical health.

The entire world rejoiced at their Moon walk. Neil Armstrong and his wife, with Mike Collins and Buzz Aldrin and their wives, spent months following their return to Earth visiting countries around the globe.

On August 13, 1969, Neil Armstrong, Buzz Aldrin, and Mike Collins and their families boarded the presidential plane *Air Force II*. Their first stop was a ticker-tape parade in New York City. They were greeted by Mayor John Lindsay and his wife, and they rode in a parade that lasted nearly an hour and a half.

Then, on to Chicago, which they felt might be a letdown after the ovation in New York, but it wasn't. The motorcade paraded down Michigan Avenue and State Street, with people hanging out of windows all along the route, throwing confetti and streamers.

After a three-and-a-half hour flight to Los Angeles, they met with President and Mrs. Nixon and their daughters, Julie and Tricia. An official state dinner was held in an enormous ballroom. After the dinner, President Nixon presented to each of the astronauts the nation's highest civilian honor, the Presidential Medal of Freedom.

On Saturday, August 16, there was a parade in Houston and an Astrodome Bonanza Show in honor of the three astronauts. The master of ceremonies was Frank Sinatra.

Finally, Neil Armstrong returned to Wapakoneta to be honored in his own hometown. The parade started at the high school and went through downtown and out to the Auglaize County Fairground for a public reception. Despite the extremely hot day, there were thousands of people lining the parade route, waving and cheering with pride. The Purdue University band marched proudly in the parade, along with the many decorated floats. Among the numerous celebrities were Bob Hope, Ed McMahon, Dr. Jonas Salk, and James Rhodes, the governor of Ohio.

The climax of these activities was their visit to Washington, D.C., where, on September 16, each of the *Apollo 11* astronauts gave a speech to a joint session of the Congress of the United States of America. Neil Armstrong said in his speech, "Responding to challenge is one of democracy's great strengths. Our successes in space lead us to hope that this strength can be used in the next decade in the solution of many of our planet's problems."

Before the astronauts' visit to Congress, they had stopped at the Washington Post Office, where they attended the unveiling of the stamp commemorating the first lunar landing. The stamp had an artist's drawing of Neil Armstrong stepping down onto the Moon's surface and a caption under the picture that said "First Man on the Moon."

At the State Department, they were given their schedule for a worldwide tour. The tour started on September 29, and they finally returned to Washington, D.C., in November, where they had dinner with the Nixons at the White House.

Their tour had taken them to Mexico City; Bogotá, Colombia; Buenos Aires, Argentina; Rio de Janeiro, Brazil; Madrid, Spain; Paris, France; Amsterdam, the Netherlands; Brussels, Belgium; Bonn and West Berlin, West Germany; London, England; Vatican City and Rome, Italy; Belgrade, Yugoslavia; Ankara, Turkey; Africa; Tehran, Iran; Bombay, India; Dacca, Bangladesh; East Pakistan; and Bangkok, Thailand. There were parades and celebrations wherever they went. They met with kings and heads of state and were honored with banquets and formal dinners.

The tour went on to Australia, where Armstrong, Aldrin, and Collins made a special stop at Perth, which was a vital link in the space program as a major tracking station. They then went to Sydney, Australia; Guam; Seoul, Korea; and their last stop before their return was in Tokyo, Japan, where they received medals of honor from the prime minister.

Neil Armstrong also received many other honors, including the Robert J. Collier Trophy in 1969; the Robert Goddard Memorial Trophy in 1970; and the Congressional Space Medal of Honor in 1978.

Armstrong worked in the NASA Office of Advanced Research until 1971, when he resigned and became a professor of aerospace engineering at the University of Cincinnati until 1979. He is now on the board of directors of several companies and enjoys living on his farm.

On the first anniversary of the Moon walk, Neil Armstrong said that he felt the message of the *Apollo* mission was that any goal can be reached, if first you identify what your goal is and then work together to reach that goal.

SPACE VOCABULARY

AERONAUTICS—the science of flight

ASCENT—to go up

CENTRIFUGE—a chamber that goes around and around to simulate little or no gravity

COLUMBIA—the spacecraft of the *Apollo 11* mission

DESCENT—to come down

EAGLE—the lunar module of the *Apollo 11* mission

GEOLOGY—the study of rocks

HATCH—the entryway into the spacecraft or lunar module

LAUNCH—the spacecraft being sent into space by the blast of a rocket

LLRV—lunar landing research vehicle, nicknamed "the Flying Bedstead"

LUNAR MODULE—the section of spacecraft

that separates from the command module to fly to the Moon

LUNAR—having to do with the Moon

MCC—mission control center

MODULE—a section of a spacecraft, which separates and operates independently

NAVIGATION—the science of traveling in space (or water)

ORBIT—circuit of a planet

RADAR—system of sending radio waves and measuring the speed of return in order to locate an object

REENTRY—when the spacecraft comes back into the atmosphere

REPLICA—an exact copy

ROCKET—the launching stage of the spacecraft that ignites and thrusts the spacecraft into space

SATELLITE—a spacecraft that flies in the orbit of the Earth

189

SEA OF TRANQUILLITY—a dry area on the Moon where the *Eagle* landed

SIMULATOR—a model of the spacecraft where the astronauts train

THRUSTERS—the jet propulsion rockets

TRAJECTORY—the path of flight

VACUUM—space without any air pressure

WEIGHTLESSNESS—no gravity

CHILDHOOD OF FAMOUS AMERICANS

The paperback biographies that you love to read!

heck off the COFAs you read.

ABIGAIL ADAMS: Girl of Colonial Days
SUSAN B. ANTHONY: Champion of Women's Rights
NEIL ARMSTRONG: Young Pilot
CRISPUS ATTUCKS: Black Leader of Colonial Patriots
CLARA BARTON: Founder of the American Red Cross
ELIZABETH BLACKWELL: Girl Doctor
DANIEL BOONE: Young Hunter and Tracker
MARGARET BOURKE-WHITE: Young Photographer
BUFFALO BILL: Frontier Daredevil
DAVY CROCKETT: Young Rifleman
ABNER DOUBLEDAY: Young Baseball Pioneer
THOMAS EDISON: Young Inventor
ALBERT EINSTEIN: Young Thinker
DWIGHT D. EISENHOWER: Young Military Leader
HENRY FORD: Young Man with Ideas
BEN FRANKLIN: Young Printer
LOU GEHRIG: One of Baseball's Greatest
HARRY HOUDINI: Young Magician
LANGSTON HUGHES: Young Black Poet
MAHALIA JACKSON: Young Gospel Singer
TOM JEFFERSON: Third President of the U.S.
HELEN KELLER: From Tragedy to Triumph

☐ JOHN FITZGERALD KENNEDY: America's Youngest President
☐ MARTIN LUTHER KING, JR.: Young Man with a Dream
☐ ROBERT E. LEE: Young Confederate
☐ ABRAHAM LINCOLN: The Great Emancipator
☐ MARY TODD LINCOLN: Girl of the Bluegrass
☐ ANNIE OAKLEY: Young Markswoman
☐ MOLLY PITCHER: Young Patriot
☐ PAUL REVERE: Boston Patriot
☐ KNUTE ROCKNEY: Young Athlete
☐ ELEANOR ROOSEVELT: Fighter for Social Justice
☐ TEDDY ROOSEVELT: Young Rough Rider
☐ BETSY ROSS: Designer of Our Flag
☐ BABE RUTH: One of Baseball's Greatest
☐ SACAGAWEA: American Pathfinder
☐ SITTING BULL: Dakota Boy
☐ JIM THORPE: Olympic Champion
☐ HARRY S. TRUMAN: Missouri Farm Boy
☐ MARK TWAIN: Young Writer
☐ GEORGE WASHINGTON: Young Leader
☐ MARTHA WASHINGTON: America's First Lady
☐ WILBUR AND ORVILLE WRIGHT: Young Fliers

COFAs are available at your favorite bookstore.

COFA (Childhood of Famous Americans)

🐘 **ALADDIN PAPERBACKS**
An imprint of Simon & Schuster Children's Publishing Division